Clara Reeve

Memoirs of Sir Roger de Clarendon, the Natural Son of Edward,

Prince of Wales,

commonly called the Black Prince: with anecdotes of many other eminent persons

of the fourteenth century. Vol. 1

Clara Reeve

Memoirs of Sir Roger de Clarendon, the Natural Son of Edward, Prince of Wales,
commonly called the Black Prince: with anecdotes of many other eminent persons of the
fourteenth century. Vol. 1

ISBN/EAN: 9783337012519

Printed in Europe, USA, Canada, Australia, Japan

Cover: Foto ©Raphael Reischuk / pixelio.de

More available books at **www.hansebooks.com**

MEMOIRS

OF

SIR ROGER DE CLARENDON.

VOL. I.

MEMOIRS

OF

SIR ROGER DE CLARENDON,

THE NATURAL SON OF

Edward Prince of Wales,

COMMONLY CALLED

THE BLACK PRINCE;

WITH

ANECDOTES OF MANY OTHER EMINENT PERSONS
OF THE FOURTEENTH CENTURY.

.BY CLARA REEVE.

In every work regard the writer's end,
Since none can compafs more than they intend;
And if the means are juft, the purpofe true,
Applaufe in fpite of trivial faults is due.
Neglect the rules each verbal critic lays,
For not to.know fome trifles is a praife.   POPE.

IN THREE VOLUMES.

VOL. I.

LONDON:
Printed for HOOKHAM and CARPENTER,
Bond-Street. 1793.

PREFACE.

"LET us now praife famous men,
" even our fathers who begat us :

" Such as bare rule in their king-
" doms, men renowned for their power,
" giving counfel by their underftand-
" ings :

" Leaders of the people by their
" counfels, and by their learning and
" wifdom, meet for [governing] the
" people, wife and eloquent in their in-
" ftructions.

A 3   " All.

" All thefe were honoured in their
" generations, and were the glory of their
" times ; and have left their names be-
" hind them."

Wifdom of the Son of Sirach.

———————

The excellent Plutarch, the prince of
hiftorians, in the firft page of the Life
of Paulus Emilius, made this valuable
remark :

" I firft undertook to write the lives
" of great men for the fervice of others,
" but I perfevere in this defign for my
" own benefit.

" The virtues of thefe illuftrious men
" are to me as a mirror, by which I
" learn to regulate my own life and con-
" duct.

" By

"By this means I enjoy the greatest
"familiarity with thefe great men; I am
"converfant with them all in turn, as
"if the fame houfe and board were
"common to us. When I read their
"hiftories, every particular virtue and
"excellence makes a deep impreffion
"upon my mind; from thence I infer
"how truly great and eftimable their
"owners muft needs have been; and
"carefully tranfcribe the moft beautiful
"and remarkable paffages of their
"lives into my own memory, as pat-
"terns for my imitation.

"A greater pleafure than this the gods
"can fcarcely grant us; nor a more cer-
"tain way to teach us virtue."—

This exemplary man fhowed by his
own conduct the effects of this noble

rule

rule which he recommends to others; and such will be produced in every virtuous and ingenuous mind, in all times and countries:—but there are a set of men in our days, who take delight in reprefenting the defects and deformities of nature. They reprefent mankind as the moft worthlefs, wicked, and miferable creatures in the whole fyftem of created beings. Their doctrines alfo produce the effects that may naturally be expected to flow from fuch a fource. They render men weak and timid, indolent and unhappy, and fometimes drive them to defpondency.

Thofe who attempt to inform and inftruct men, fhould give them fuch a degree of confidence in themfelves, as is neceffary to encourage them to exert

their

their abilities, and urge them to prefs
forward to obtain the prize of their labours; for virtue requires induftry and
activity in her difciples; they muft perfevere in fpite of dangers and difficulties,
and go on till they reach the fummit of
perfection. The man who thinks himfelf
unable and unworthy to climb this hill
that leads to the temple of virtue, will
hardly have the courage neceffary to
climb it; after a few ineffectual attempts
and difcouragements, he will fink into
indolence and defpondency, and remain
at the bottom of the hill all the remainder of his life.

When we contemplate the great actions which men like ourfelves, with the
fame paffions and weakneffes, were able
to perform, we fay to ourfelves, furely

A 5　　　　　　　we

we ought not to defpair of equalling them !—No, we will endeavour to furpafs them.

If the courage of Alexander, the continence of Scipio, the clemency of Titus, the truly royal virtues of Trajan, and the two firft Antonines, had had the power to ftimulate the youth of all times and countries, to imitate their great examples, how much more do the actions of great men of their own country work upon their tender and flexible minds, and infpire them with a more ardent defire to imitate, and excel them ! We refpect the climate, the air, the foil, and every thing that contributed to produce and fofter fuch men ; we believe that they muft of neceffity produce a fuccef-fion of them, and that ourfelves fhall

place

place our names in the rolls of fame, among thofe who have done honour to our country.

If by fome men this fhould be called a prejudice, I anfwer, happy are the ftates where fuch prejudices remain! where they are not done away by falfe philofophy, and falfe refinements: where that is the cafe, it may fairly be concluded, that nation's glory and happinefs is on the decline.

We know that heaven is impartial in its difpenfations, that it has given bleffings peculiar to every nation upon the face of the earth. We know that there have been illuftrious men of all times and countries, whofe names have defcended to us, wherever there were men able to record their actions; for this is

A 6   the

the true æra of hiftory, and thefe men are equally neceffary to each other.

Britain may juftly boaft of the great men fhe has produced; fhe may vie with any nation under the cope of heaven. When we read of our glorious anceftors, their actions ought to ftimulate us to equal them, to fupport and maintain the honour of our country: to be afhamed to degenerate from our forefathers, to fit down in indolence and effeminacy, and bring reproach upon them.

This earth of majefty, this feat of Mars,
This other Eden, demi-paradife;
This fortrefs built by nature for herfelf,
Againft infection and the hand of war;
This happy breed of men, this little world.—
This precious ftone fet in the filver fea,

Which

Which serves it in the office of a wall;
Or as a moat defensive to an house,
Against the envy of less happy lands.
This land of noble souls, this dear, dear land,
Dear for her reputation through the world;
Britain bound in with the triumphant siege
Of watery Neptune. Let it not be said,
That Britain, which was wont to conquer others,
Hath made a shameful conquest of herself.

SHAKESPEARE.

Our warriors, our statesmen, our poets, our philosophers, make of themselves a list of famous men, worthy the study of all the world, and they are translated into all languages.

While other countries do honour to the worthies of our's, it is more particularly the duty of every son of Britain to know them well, to be thoroughly informed

formed in the annals of his country. This fhould enforce the leffon of the excellent Plutarch, and produce the fame effects that fuch reading did upon his mind.

In the hiftory of mankind, there have been certain æras, remarkable for the production of great men. Whether thefe have been owing to natural or accidental caufes remains a problem, and we can only raife conjectures concerning it.

Princes of eminent virtues and abilities have always drawn great men around them; and this is a criterion of their characters.

But again; republics have at leaft as frequently brought individuals into notice and celebrity. The many petty ftates into which ancient Greece was divided,

vided, produced a number of men wor
thy to be immortalized by the pen of
the incomparable Plutarch. The Roman hiſtory is a ſeries of the lives and
actions of great men. Rome was never·
greater than in the interval between the
firſt Triumvirate, and the final eſtabliſh-
ment of the Imperial ſtate ; ſhe produced more great men in a ſhorter ſpace
of time.

There will always be found men to
contemplate and admire the lives and
actions of great men, as they ſtill reſpect
the ſtatues and pictures of them, though
they no longer aſpire to imitate them.

The age of King Edward IIId was
one of thoſe moſt fruitful of eminent
men, not only in England, but in all
the countries of Europe ;—it is an æra
deſerving our reſpect and admiration.

The

The writer of the following sheets
once aspired to write a history of all the
great men that lived in this reign; she
filled several sheets with names only;
she found the undertaking too great for
her strength, and gave over the design.
Still there remained a wish to snatch the
names of the principal worthies of this
age from oblivion, and to give a new
impression of them to the present times.

She had beside this another stimulus,
to give a faithful picture of a well-governed kingdom, wherein a true subor-
dination of ranks and degrees was observed, and of a great prince at the head
of it.

The new philosophy of the present
day avows a levelling principle, and de-
clares that a state of anarchy is more

beauti-

beautiful than that of order and regula-
rity. There is nothing more likely to
convince mankind of the errors of thefe
men, than to fet before them examples
of good government, and warnings of
the mifchievous confequences of their
own principles.

For forms of government let fools conteft,
Whate'er is beft adminifter'd is beft.—POPE.

All human fyftems are imperfect, all
forms of government are defective, liable to fall into error and miftake, but
capable of being rectified. That is the
beft government and moft likely to be
permanent, that makes different ranks
and degrees of men neceffary to each
other, and leads them to co-operate together

gether in order to promote the good of the whole.

May defpotifm be for ever abolifhed ! —May a juft and benevolent fyftem rife upon its ruins!—But a form of government founded upon levelling principles, never did, nor ever can continue. Rome had a gradation of ranks during her republican ftate ; fhe had her patricians, her equites, her plebeians, befide the fub-divifion of the public offices, which were equivalent to a minuter gradation.

If the populace are allowed to overturn the government, and by their wifdom frame a new conftitution, they will foon find it defective, and by the fame right fet afide the firft, and fabricate a fecond, and a third, and fo on: how can

there.

there be any thing permanent in fuch a
ftate ?

<blockquote>

Who deferves greatnefs,
Deferves your hate, for your affections are
A fick man's appetite, who defires moft
What would increafe his evil. . He that depends
Upon your favours, fwims with fins of lead,
And hews down oaks with rufhes. Hang ye—
    truft ye !
With every minute you do change your mind,
And call him noble that was now your hate,
Him vile that was your garland.

SHAKESPEARE.
</blockquote>

We have feen lately fuch a fucceffion
of favourites of the public in a neigh-
bour country, fo have they paffed away
like fmoke, new ones have fucceeded,
a general diftruft has taken place, and
thofe

thofe who ferve them beft, are liable to their moft fevere refentment and cruelty. Let Britain fhudder at the fcene before her, and grafp her bleffings the clofer.

I have endeavoured to fhow princes and heroes as men, not as angels; compofed of great qualities mixed with human infirmities, capable of virtue, but liable to error, yet upon the whole men worthy of our refpect and imitation.

Many attempts have been made of late years to build fictitious ftories upon hiftorical names and characters; the foundations were bad, and the ftructures have fallen down.

To falfify hiftorical facts and characters is a kind of facrilege againft thofe great names upon which hiftory has affixed

fixed the feal of truth. The confequences are mifchievous; it mifleads
young minds eager in the fearch of
truth, and enthufiafts in the purfuit of
thofe virtues which are the objects of
their admiration, upon whom one true
character has more effect than a thoufand fictions.

It is to thefe young and ingenuous
minds that I write; minds yet uncon-
taminated by the vile indolence, effeminacy, and extravagance of modern life
and manners. For them have I framed
a ftory that does not in any refpect contradict the annals of hiftory; which may
entertain their minds without corrupting
their hearts.

Thofe characters with whom I have
taken fome liberties, are fuch as are
barely

barely named in hiftory, and have left room to fay juft what I pleafed. Such is that of Sir Roger de Clarendon, who, though he gives name to the work, is by no means the principal character.

Who fpoke in parables I need not fay,
But fure he knew it was a pleafant way,
Sound fenfe by plain examples to convey.—
Alfo in Heathen authors we may find,
That pleafure with inftruction fhould be join'd;
So take the grain, and leave the chaff behind.

If reflecting upon thefe faint fketches of illuftrious characters fhould ftimulate a few readers to imitate thofe virtues they can admire;—if comparing ancient manners with modern ones they fhould perceive the defects of both,

and

and that the boaftings of the prefent times of their fuperiority, are not fo well founded as many believe:—if furveying both with candour and impartiality, they fhould feleƈt the good and reform the evil—this will be a noble reward for the labour and induftry of the author :— then will fhe take leave of the public with the fentence of the Roman aƈtor:

Valete et Plaudite!

HIS-

HISTORIANS *consulted in this* WORK.

FROISSART--WALSINGHAM—HOLLINSHED
—HALL—STOW—HARDING—SPEED—
BAKER — JOSHUA BARNES — RAPIN—
SMOLLET.—

THE

MEMOIRS

OF

Sir ROGER de CLARENDON.

GREAT and good princes refemble the fun
in all its glory, which warms and brightens
every object within the circle of its attrac-
tion : the rays extend on all fides : they dry
up the noxious vapours that hover under-
neath, and, by a powerful kind of magnetifm, attract merit of all kinds, and bring it
within their own vortex.

When the great King Edward the Third
kept his court at London, and his renowned
fon Edward, Prince of Wales and Aquitain,
kept his court at Bourdeaux, men of fuperior
abilities in all arts, fciences, and profeffions,

came from all parts of Europe to ferve under
their banners, and to enjoy a fhelter from the
ftorms of fortune under their glorious patronage and protection, and they reflected back
again the fplendor they derived from their
illuftrious protectors.—Princes of mean abilities and narrow hearts are jealous of thofe
who have greater underftandings and knowledge than themfelves; but it is the glory of
a good king to be furrounded by a circle of
eminent men, fome who can affift him in all
his fchemes for the good of his people, and
others who can record his virtues, and both
together will compofe for him a wreath of
immortality.—The Prince of Wales was attended by a band of gentlemen of all countries, who were called Knights-companions;
they were his defence in war, and the ornament of his court in peace; they amounted
to between five and fix thoufand men. Sir
Hugh de Calverly was one of thefe knights;
he was of undaunted courage and fidelity,
and was well acquainted with all the arts of
peace: he was high in favour with both the
King and the Prince of Wales. In the latter
end of the reign of King Edward he was governor of Calais, and defended it gallantly
                                    againft

againſt open force and ſecret treachery; he
continued in this office till the death of the
King.

Edward the Black Prince, ſo called from
the terror his arms inſpired, died before his
father, to the irreparable grief and loſs of
the Engliſh nation : he was equally lamented by his ſubjects in Guienne, and both
countries united in making his eulogy. He
was the hero of his age; no man ſo terrible
in war, none ſo generous and gentle in his
own court, and to his friends and followers.
He never fought a battle he did not win, yet
his modeſty and courteſy excelled even his
valour.

He poſſeſſed all the ſocial and domeſtic
virtues; he was ſober, continent, and tem-
perate in all things : the only blemiſh in his
character was too great a fondneſs for military
glory, which he ſhewed in aſſiſting Don Pedro the Cruel to recover the crown of Caſtile and Leon, a man truly deteſtable for his
cruelty and injuſtice. He effected this de-
ſign, but the heats of Spain affected his con-
ſtitution, and he caught the diſtemper there
that brought him to his grave.

En-

England embraced in her arms, and in her heart, the only furviving fon of this beloved prince, Richard of Bourdeaux. The Commons petitioned the King to grant him all the honours of his father, and he was immediately created Prince of Wales, Duke of Cornwall, and Earl of Chefter. Within a year after, he fucceeded his grandfather, being but in the twelfth year of his age.

This young prince afcended the throne with the warmeft affection and wifhes of all the people. He was beautiful in his perfon, courteous in his manners, and his fubjects believed they faw in him the heir of his father's virtues and fine qualities: but time and experience fhowed them the contrary, and deftroyed all their hopes and expectations, and their refpect and confidence in him. During the minority of the king, his government was refpectable, from the abilities of his uncles, John of Ghent duke of Lancafter, Edmund of Langley duke of York, and Thomas of Wodeftock duke of Gloucefter. The young King was impatient to hold the reins of government, but as foon as he was in poffeffion of them, his weaknefs and infufficiency became apparent

to

to all men. He was light and vain-glorious, fickle and inconstant, fond of shews, and pageants, and vanities of every kind. His uncles endeavoured to restrain his youthful follies, but he rejected their counsels, despised their admonitions, and acted in defiance of them. He drew about him a set of venal and profligate favorites, and squandered away upon them the revenues of his kingdom. His subjects, at the beginning, were fond of him to excess; they readily gave him an increase of revenue, and supplied him with the means to support his dignity. He was always in want of money, and contriving new means to obtain it. Whenever he had wheedled or exacted new subsidies from his parliament, under promises of reformation and œconomy, no sooner was the money received, than the promises were broken, and he plunged again into the same course of dissipation and prodigality. By this absurd and foolish conduct he lost, by degrees, the confidence and affections of his people. After a long series of contests with the barons, who were then the guardians of the people's liberties, and perpetual disputes with his parliament, he became the object

of

of their hatred and contempt. They invited his kinfman, Henry of Bolingbroke, whom Richard had injured in the higheſt degree, by driving him into exile and feizing on his inheritance, to come to their affiſtance. They got the perſon of Richard into their power, they exhibited a folemn charge againſt him in a free and full parliament, they obliged him to fign the inſtrument of his own depoſition, and placed Henry duke of Lancaſter upon the throne, who was the next *male heir* of the houſe of Plantagenet. This is an awful leſſon to princes, how they abuſe the confidence of their people.

The fubject of the following ſtory bears frequent reference to the hiſtory of this un-fortunate reign, and will afford matter for remarks on paſt times, and compariſons with the preſent.

During the firſt conteſts between King Richard and his people, Sir Hugh Calverly was one of the moſt faithful and moſt re-ſpectable adherents to the King. He loved him for the fake of his illuſtrious father and grandfather; he hoped that time and experi-ence would teach him to correct his errors, and that the latter part of his reign would make

make atonement for the former : in this hope he withstood the association of the barons, and steadily adhered to the King. Sir Hugh commanded the English army in the only action that did honour to this inglorious reign. He assisted the Bishop of Norwich in his absurd campaign against the Count of Flanders ; he defeated the Count in the field, and supported the Bishop with credit and success : but their triumph was short ; fortune soon after declared against them ; the French came to the Count's assistance. The English, weakened by repeated losses, were obliged to retreat to Calais, from whence they wrote to ask a speedy re-inforcement from the King, or else they must shortly return home.—Richard talked highly ; he threatened revenge against the Count of Flanders, and the King of France his ally. He promised to send an army immediately, under the command of his uncle, the Duke of Lancaster, but his valour evaporated in words. He was so tardy in his preparations, that before they were ready to embark, the truce was expired. The Bishop and his party were obliged to accept the terms offered by the King of France ; they returned to

En-

England with the wreck of their army, covered with difgrace, in lieu of their former
glory. Sir Hugh Calverly was afhamed of
his party and fituation; he refolved from
that time to refide in his native country,
and to limit his fervices to the perfon of his
King, and to fupport him againft his enemies at home. Sir Hugh Calverly from this
time lived at Calverly-hall, in the bofom of
his family, with his beloved wife and children. He had married a lady of the Bour-
chier family, endowed with many virtues
and fine qualities. She had brought him fe-
ven children, five of which lived to the age
of maturity, two fons and three daughters,
which were all promifing children at this
time we are fpeaking of. The eldeft fon
was already knighted by the King, whofe
caufe he had efpoufed againft the party of the
barons. This young gentleman often jour-
neyed between London and Calverly-hall;
he was endowed with many noble qualities,
dutiful to his parents, and affectionate to all
his family. Lionel, the younger fon, was
yet a boy, and the darling of his parents, and
all the reft of the family. The daughters
were young, virtuous, and amiable; we fhall

fpeak

speak of their peculiar qualities hereafter. Sir Hugh was a moſt tender huſband and affectionate father; he was beloved and reſpected by his neighbours, tenants, and dependents; he was an exemplary landlord, friend, and maſter. After a youth of military ſervice, and glory dearly earned, he hoped to enjoy an old age of honour and repoſe in his native country, with his wiſe and children. This noble and renowned knight was taken away from his family at the age of fifty and five years, by an epidemical fever, which raged in the year 1386. He died too ſoon for his family, but, perhaps, not for himſelf; he eſcaped the troubles of his country, which he muſt have ſhared, and in which he might have ſuffered in his perſon, honours, and fortune.

His eldeſt ſon, Sir John Calverly, inherited his father's fortune, and his virtues. He was loyal to his king and country, affectionate to his mother and family, and looked upon his brother and ſiſters as his children whom he was bound to protect and ſupport.

As ſoon as the funeral duties were performed, and the firſt poignancy of grief was abated, Lady Calverly propoſed to leave the

family

family feat, and to retire to a fmaller houfe upon her own paternal eftate, which fhe had preferved for herfelf in cafe fhe fhould be left a widow; or for her daughters, whenever her eldeft fon fhould marry.

Sir John befought her earneftly to ftay at Calverly-hall, faying, he wifhed to enjoy her company and that of his fifters, and alfo he hoped to receive much benefit from her refidence there, and from her advice and af-fiftance in regulating and governing his family.

The good lady confented to ftay with her fon fome time longer, upon condition that he fhould be looking out for a wife in the mean time; faying, it was his duty to pre-ferve and continue a family that was an ho-nour to its country, and a bleffing to its de-pendents.

Sir John agreed to this condition, and my Lady faid, fhe would not leave him till that happy period fhould arrive.

Lady Calverly educated her daughters in that retired and virtuous referve, which in thofe days was thought a duty. It was be-lieved neceffary for the guard and protection of female virtue. In thofe times young

1   maid-

maidens were feldom feen out of their mother's prefence : it would have been thought a breach of virgin modefty.

The filent and retired virtues were cultivated, modefty, humility, and complacency ; virtues that were in due time to be a bleffing to the men who fhould be their hufbands ; they were likewife taught thofe ufeful qualities which fhould render them capable of fuperintending a well-governed family.

Madam Ifabel, the eldeft daughter, was generally reckoned handfome ; fhe was tall and well made, but proud and ftately, vain of her beauty and family. She was ambitious of making a great alliance, that fhould reflect honour upon her family, and render herfelf the firft perfon in it. The brave and gentle, the modeft and deferving Clement Woodville, fighed in fecret for this haughty beauty. He was the moft intimate and beloved friend and companion of Sir John Calverly. His father was an officer of great courage and reputation, who had faved the life of Sir Hugh Calverly in the field, and loft his own in performing that gallant action. From that day Sir Hugh adopted his children for his own, and took them into

his

his own family. This brave gentleman left two sons and a daughter; the last-named was placed in a convent, Lady Calverly designed her for the veil, for she had particular objections to receiving her into her family.

The second daughter of Lady Calverly was called Edith; she was not generally thought so handsome as Isabel'; it was necessary that she should be known before she was admired; but then her virtues and graces seemed to illuminate her person, and the beholders wondered that they had not always perceived her to be beautiful: the oftener she was seen, the more charming she appeared; and those who once loved her, were sure to love her always.

Edith saw and heard the sighs of Clement Woodville for her sister; she was sensible of his merits; she felt for him the pride and disdain with which he was treated, and thrown to the utmost distance: she endeavoured by her gentleness and courtesy to comfort him for the mortifications he received from Isabel. Thus, while she thought she was only doing justice to injured merit, the fair Edith, unawares to herself, pointed

the

the dart of love againſt her own tender and generous heart. She felt an intereſt in every thing that related to Clement, and, indeed, all the cares and anxieties of a lover, always implied but never expreſſed.

Clement's firſt attentions to Edith were dictated by pure gratitude and reſpect; he never dreamed that love was ſtealing into his heart under the guiſe of generous friendſhip, which he might ſafely admit and indulge.

Theſe characters will in due time unfold themſelves more fully; let us now ſpeak of the youngeſt daughter of Lady Calverly: ſhe was baptized by the name of Amabel, but by her mother and family called by the diminutive of Mabel; ſhe was ſeven years younger than Iſabel, and three than Edith; ſhe was at the time we ſpeak of, juſt entered into her fourteenth year. Mabel was the bud of beauty, which promiſed to expand hereafter; ſhe was lively, ingenuous, and engaging; ſhe knew no reaſon for concealing her thoughts, therefore ſhe uttered them without reſerve.

In thoſe days, mothers thought it their duty to check their daughters, when they diſcovered an over-lively diſpoſition; levity

of

of temper was thought to indicate fomething wrong in the head or the heart; they feared it would lead them into error from mifcon-duct, and finally to punifhment.

Mabel was talkative, curious, and inquifi-tive; fhe was defired to liften more, and to fpeak lefs. Urfula, an old fervant of Lady Calverly's, was appointed governefs to Mabel; fhe inftructed her in all kinds of needle-work, and fhe was ordered to reftrain her immoderate love of talking. Urfula defired her to wear in her heart a certain proverb; "Maids fhould be feen, but not heard." Mabel thought this a hard faying, but fhe had no refource; fhe was obliged to bury her thoughts in her own bofom till night fet her tongue at liberty. She flept with her fifter Edith, whofe gentlenefs and affection permitted her to unburden her mind, and to prattle as much as fhe pleafed, which was till fleep locked up all her faculties, and laid her tongue to reft.—Mabel ufed to dream fre-quently, which proved that her mind was not idle while her body repofed; fhe always told her fifter her dreams as foon as fhe waked; this was her amufement till Urfula called her to rife, and Edith fometimes fufpected

pected she dreamed waking as well as sleeping. Mabel used to dream of fine houses, delightful gardens full of flowers and fruits, shady bowers full of singing birds, and murmuring streams; sometimes she dreamed of strict mothers, proud sisters, and cross governesses; she had not yet begun to dream of knights or 'squires; but we shall find, that in due time her reveries wanted no kind of embellishment.

Edith frequently advised her to leave off telling her dreams and fancies; but, she said, she could not forbear doing it, it relieved her mind, and, in short, it was the greatest pleasure of her life.

Sir John Calverly was fond of his sisters and brother; Mabel and Lionel were his favourites; he would set them upon his knees, and caress them like a father, and they loved him as if he was really so. He liked to hear Mabel prattle, and she was happy in the indulgence, till my lady was tired of hearing her; she used then to send Mabel to her governess, and reproved Sir John for indulging her propensity to talk overmuch.

Sir John used frequently to make journeys to and from London; he had recommended

mended Richard Woodville, Clement's elder brother, to the notice of the Earl of Suffolk, one of the King's greateft favourites; by his intereft he was appointed one of the King's houfehold fervants, and he was afterwards promoted to be one of his attendants on the King's perfon.

Clement Woodville frequently attended Sir John in his journeys; he faw and converfed with his brother, who wifhed to place him near himfelf, and to keep him at court. Clement's opinions were different; he was more inclined to take the fide of the Barons than that of the King. Richard was a warm royalift; he thought the King could do nothing wrong: he looked upon him as the landlord of the kingdom, and that the lives, liberties, and properties of the fubjects, were all at his difpofal. He afked his brother, whether he expected to gain preferment by joining with thofe who prefumed to check the King and to limit his expences, I would fooner do fo, replied Clement, than join with thofe who flatter and miflead him, to his own ruin, and that of the kingdom. Go to them, faid Richard, but expect neither friendfhip nor preferment from me, unlefs

you

you alter your opinions, and confent to fail
with the tide of the times.

The following year the Earl of Suffolk
was impeached in parliament of high crimes
and mifdemeanors againft the ftate; he was
convicted of them in the prefence of the
King, who publicly reproved him, and confented to his imprifonment. He was committed to the cuftody of the Duke of Gloucefter, who, as high conftable of the kingdom, fent him prifoner to Windfor-caftle.
The parliament appointed a committee of
eleven noblemen to infpect the revenue of
the crown ever fince the King's acceffion to
the throne, and to reform all the abufes of
the late adminiftration, and the King fwore
folemnly to abide by their decifion.

Sir John Calverly was of the King's council at this time; he advifed him to endeavour
to recover the confidence and affection of
his people, and to agree to what the parliament propofed; he hoped by this meafure
that peace and harmony would be reftored
between the King and his people. The parliament, fatisfied with this redrefs of grievances,
hoped to fee better days in future; they con-
fided in the new adminiftration; they broke

up,

up, and returned to their refpective homes, fatisfied and happy. Sir John fent Clement Woodville to Calverly-hall, to defire his mother to make preparations for the reception of feveral gentlemen his friends, whom he fhould bring home with him to celebrate the feftival of Chriftmas, which was juft approaching.

In thofe days, Chriftmas was kept as fo folemn a feftival ought to be. The nobility and gentry of this land entertained their friends, neighbours, and tenants, with great munificence and hofpitality, though, perhaps, not fo much luxury, as has been feen in later times, when every day in the week is kept as a feftival, not indeed to God, or to man, but to certain pagan deities, called Bacchus and Venus.

In the good old times, Charity extended her hands, fhe fed the hungry, fhe clothed the naked, fhe fent firing and bedding to all thofe that ftood in need of them, fhe cheered the afflicted heart, and bade all her children rejoice at that facred commemoration, which proclaimed, " *Glory to God in the higheft, and* " *on earth peace, and good will towards men.*"— The ladies of the family of Calverly thought them-

themfelves well employed in making preparations to receive their guefts, and providing
for their entertainment and accommodation.

Sir John and his friends came to Calverly-
hall three days before Chriftmas ; I will only
mention the names of the principal guefts.
Sir Oliver de Marney, Sir Michael Bretten-
ham, Sir William Truffel, Sir Reginald Cobham, eldeft fon to the Lord Cobham, with
feveral other young gentleman of family and
fortune. Sir John Calverly defired the company of his mother and fifters at his table.
The good lady was fcrupulous about bringing her daughters into men's company, but
her fon infifted on it. He told her, that he
was proud of his fifters ; that he wifhed them
to be feen, as a ftep to their being married in
due time ; that he brought with him a fet of
gallant bachelors, out of which fhe might
choofe a fon-in-law, or, perhaps, more, and
fuch as would do honour to the family.

My Lady made objections to introducing
her daughters, left it fhould be fufpected fhe
had any fuch expectations. Sir John faid,
he would take all that imputation upon himfelf; he laughed at her fcruples. My Lady
retired,

retired, faying, it was not fo in her young days.

They celebrated the feftival with becoming folemnity; the day after, Lady Calverly invited a neighbouring family to meet her guefts, Sir Hugh Burleigh and his Lady, with two fons and four daughters; fhe thought the other young ladies' company would leffen the impropriety of that of her daughters: fhe wifhed one of them might captivate her fon, and fhe had laid her eye upon the eldeft fon for one of her daughters. Thefe thoughts proceeded from the beft of motives; fhe wifhed that her children might fettle near her, that fhe might fee them frequently.

They had a fumptuous dinner in the great hall, without any carpet under their feet, or lifting upon the doors; but they had a noble fire, with part of the body of an old tree behind, and logs of all fizes piled round it. There was no noify or diforderly mirth, but there was cheerfulnefs and decorum. After dinner the ladies retired into a large parlour, wainfcotted with Englifh oak, and ornamented with the portraits of the anceftors of the Calverly family. The gentlemen

foon.

foon followed them; they rofe from table with cool heads, warm hearts, and light heels; they thought themfelves honoured to touch the hands of a fair lady, and to lead her into the dance. They had neither tea nor coffee, but cakes and comfets, with light and pleafant wines, chiefly made at home, and plenty of good Englifh beer.

This noble company dined at twelve o'clock, fupped at fix, and danced till twelve, which in thofe days was called midnight; and it was only at Chriftmas holidays that they ever fet up fo late.

They rofe by candle light the next morning, they were fummoned to breakfaft at eight o'clock; there were cold pafties, hams, and tongues, with cold roafted meats, and good beer; afterwards they met in the family chapel and worfhipped God, after which they had converfation parties at home, or riding parties abroad. There were neither coaches, nor chaifes, nor phaetons, nor curricles; but every lady had her palfrey, and every one a gentleman, who called himfelf her fervant, to attend and protect her; they rode with wind, rain, or fnow in their faces, and were not afraid of the air of their own country.

try. The family of Burleigh ſtaid two nights
at Calverly-hall; on the third day they returned home, after inviting all the company
to return their viſit in the following week.

After their departure, in one of the inter-
vals between breakfaſt and dinner, as the
young ladies were ſitting in my Lady's
apartment, and amuſing themſelves with
their needlework, Lady Calverly ſpoke of
the gentlemen who honoured Calverly-hall
with their company; ſhe found ſomething
to commend in all of them; ſhe aſked her
eldeſt daughter her opinion of the perſons
and merits of ſeveral of them. " If, Iſa-
" bel, you were to chooſe an huſband from
" among them, tell me which you would
" prefer." The young lady bluſhed—after
ſome minutes' ſilence ſhe ſpoke: " Why,
" really Madam, I have not thought of any
" ſuch thing; but, I believe, if I were to
" chooſe one, it would be him who is heir
" to a title and a great fortune."—" Oh fie,
" Iſabel! I am ſorry to hear that ambi-
" tion governs you; it is a man's merit ra-
" ther than his rank, that ſhould entitle
" him to a young lady's favour."—" So I
" think," ſaid Edith.—" Yes," ſaid my
Lady,

Lady, " but I mean always that he muſt be
" a *gentleman* who pretends to a lady of fa-
" mily."—" I underſtand it ſo," ſaid Edith.
—" Madam," ſaid Iſabel, " you have raiſed
" my curioſity, will you not gratify it ?"—
" I will in part ; there is a gentleman in this
" company at our houſe, who has caſt an
" eye of partiality upon you, Iſabel; but it
" is not he that is heir to a Baron's title : he
" does you and the family honour; but I
" will not at this time tell you who he is,
" to mortify your vanity."—" That is ra-
" ther cruel of you, Madam ; but I will en-
" deavour to correct my curioſity, ſince you
" are not diſpoſed to indulge it."—

Iſabel ſtood corrected : the two younger
ladies looked earneſtly at their mother; they
ſeemed deſirous to know farther particulars.
" My dear girls," ſaid my Lady, " you
" ſhall know every thing in proper time.
" Mabel, your eyes ſparkle with curioſity,
" mind your work, and learn to ſuppreſs it ;
" for it is not neceſſary that you ſhould be
" the firſt to know every thing of conſe-
" quence in the family."—Mabel thought it
very hard that her eyes might not aſk queſ-
tions when her tongue was quiet. Edith
ſmiled

fmiled but was filent; but fhe thought on fomething that was not unpleafing to her.

My Lady fuffered fome days to pafs without gratifying the curiofity fhe had raifed. Sir John was impatient to prefent a fervant to his fifter; he inquired whether fhe was informed of the important conqueft fhe had made. She anfwered, that her mother had told her enough to make her wifh to know more, but had refufed to explain it at that time. Sir John broke the ice at once, and told her it was Sir William Truffel. He expatiated upon his family, fortune, and merit, and faid, fhe ought to think herfelf honoured by the propofal. Ifabel referred to her mother, and Sir John went directly to her apartments, where he learned the reafons of my Lady's delay, and was fatisfied of the caufe of it. The day following he introduced Sir William Truffel to his fifter, who received him in a ftately manner, and feemed to expect the homage due to a princefs. The lover was not pleafed with his reception; he complained of the difdain and cruelty of the lady. Sir John encouraged him to perfift. My Lady was defired to ufe her influence. Another interview paffed; ftill fhe

was

was high and fcornful. The mother interroga-
ted her; had fhe any particular diflike to Sir
William ?—No.—Why then did fhe behave
fo proudly to him ?—Ifabel faid, he was almoft a ftranger to her, and that he ought to
wait her time : that fhe might, perhaps,
have better offers, and fhe was not in a hurry.—My Lady checked this idea; fhe told
her, that woman did not deferve a worthy
hufband, who could keep a gentleman in
fufpenfe from fuch a motive ; that fhe would
not allow fuch principles to govern any
child of her's; and finally, that fhe muft either accept Sir William, or elfe give him a
proper denial and difmifs him entirely.—
Ifabel faid, that men were unreafonable creatures; that if fhe had accepted him at the firft
offer, he might have thought her too forward, and that was worfe than being thought
too coy.—My Lady defired her to confider
well before fhe rejeded him, that fhe was
not likely to have a better offer, and if fhe
had no diflike to him, gratitude fhould infpire her with affedion for the man who had
diftinguifhed her from all other women, and
offered her his hand, heart, and fortune.—

VOL. I.   C   Ifa-

Ifabel confidered the matter again; fhe thought better of it—fhe reflected that hufbands were not offered every day, and that a prefent good was preferable to a future contingency. At the next interview with Sir William fhe was more gracious to him, and in every fucceeding interview fhe became more compliable. In ten days after, Sir William declared his wifhes and his hopes to all the company. The report circulated through every part of the family, it reached the ear of Clement Woodville, and from thence ftruck his heart like the feathered arrow of a crofs-bow. He pined inwardly, he loft his appetite and reft, and took to his bed. The family were fo engroffed by their company, and the defired match, that his ficknefs was not fo much obferved as it would have been at any other time. Edith foon had knowledge of it: fhe felt his forrows, and gueffed the caufe of his illnefs; fhe daily inquired after his health, and fent him friendly meffages.

The family and their guefts returned the vifit of the Burleigh family, Mabel was thought too young to be one of the party. Edith complained of the tooth-ach and defired

fired to be left at home. How far it was
real is not eafy to determine, but fhe certainly preferred ftaying at home to all the propofed pleafures of the vifit to Burleigh-
houfe. The heir of that family had made
fome advances towards her; had paid her
very pointed attentions. She difliked him,
and was glad to avoid his company. After
the company were fet out, Edith fent her
maid to inquire after the health of Mafter
Clement, for fo he was called in the family.
Jane had every day received and returned
meffages between thefe two friends. Edith
wifhed to fee him, but would not be guilty
of the impropriety of going to his apartment.
She ordered Jane to afk whether he was well
enough to walk down into the parlour,
where the family ufed to meet when alone.

Edith and her fifter Mabel walked in the
garden; it was a clear frofty day, a fine
blue fky, and the fun deigned to illuminate
the fcene. Thefe young ladies had no idea
of being afraid of the cold; they walked
above an hour, and came in warm and re-
frefhed.

As they entered the hall Clement met
them; he looked pale and fickly, but endea-

voured

voured to appear cheerful. Edith was
doubtful how to addrefs him, Mabel faved
her the trouble. " Oh dear, how glad I
" am to fee you well enough to leave your
" room! how do you, Mr. Clement ?"—
Clement bowed and thanked her. " I am
" better, I hope, and I am defirous to pay
" my acknowledgements to you, ladies, for
" your very kind inquiries after a man, who
" has almoft thought himfelf forgotten by
" all befide you."—" That is impoffible;"
faid Edith, " every body has been concerned
" for you; but Sir John has been fo much
" engaged that he could not fee you fo often
" as he wifhed; but he loves and pities you."
—" I ought not to doubt it, Madam. I am,
" indeed, comforted by your goodnefs to me,
" and I will ftrive to deferve it."—" Then
" ftrive to be well, Sir; I wifh I knew of
" any thing that would do you good."—
" Your compaffion, Madam, is a powerful
" medicine; I feel the effects of it. How
" can a man be entirely wretched when the
" fair Edith pities and relieves him?"—
" And pray," fays Mabel, " does not my
" pity do you as much good as my fifter's?"—
" You are very good, my dear young lady,
" I am

" I am inexpreffibly obliged to you both."—
" If you defire to oblige us in return," faid
Edith, " caft away care and melancholy, be
" well and cheerful. Do yourfelf the juf-
" tice to believe, that if there are fome peo-
" ple that neglect and flight your merit,
" there are others who regard you more for
" this very reafon."—" That is moft fweetly
" faid, Madam ; I will make your friendfhip
" my only remedy ; I will wear it next my
" heart, and I believe, I truft it will cure
" me."—Edith blufhed and felt confufed, fhe
feared fhe had fpoken too freely ; fhe took
her fifter's hand, curtfied, and withdrew.
She left Clement with an improved afpect,
his eye was brightened, and his heart cheered.
She heard him fay, as we went from him,
" I will no more defpair of peace and hap-
" pinefs, fince an angel deigns to be my com-
" forter."

" It feems to me," faid Mabel, " that
" your pity does him more good than mine,
" and I cannot find out the reafon of it."—
" There is no reafon to be found, my dear ;
" his gratitude is equal to us both, and he
" only names me firft as being the elder fif-
" ter."—" Oh, that is it then ! I hope I

" fhall

" fhall in time have my fhare of people's
" gratitude and politenefs, but at prefent
" my elder fifters feem to take it all to them-
" felves; all the gentlemen bow, and com-
" pliment, and make fine fpeeches to you and
" Ifabel, but they treat me like a child.
" Well, perhaps one day it may be my turn."
—Edith fmiled; fhe begged her to have patience, and it would come to her turn foon
enough. They went to their own apartment; they plied their needles with Urfula
till they were called to dinner. Clement
did not come down to dinner that day; they
walked again in the afternoon till it grew
dufkifh. Edith's tooth-ach was finely abated:
Mabel prattled as much as fhe pleafed, and
they went to reft in perfect health and cheerfulnefs.

The next morning Jane was fent with her
ufual meffage to Mafter Clement. She
brought word that he had a good night's reft,
and was finely to-day; that he wifhed to
fpeak with Madam Edith alone; and he
would meet her in the dining parlour an hour
before dinner. Edith had fome difficulty to
amufe Mabel, and to make her go another
way; fhe fixed her at laft, and was more
than

than punctual to her appointment. She waited a quarter of an hour before Clement arrived, he apologized for losing so many minutes of her company ; she excused herself for coming before the time, fearing they should be interrupted by Mabel.

Clement begged pardon for the liberty he was about to take, but her goodness had encouraged him to open his heart to her. He confessed that he had loved Madam Isabel too much for his peace, but he had never made her any positive declaration of it. He knew she had perceived the secret of his heart, by the disdain she had shewn him, which before time she was not wont to do, for of late she had not behaved with common civility, but had treated him like a slave, not worthy of her notice : he confessed that his folly had deserved the punishment, and that when he heard of the proposed marriage, it quite overcame him, but that he was now resolved to get the better of it : that he begged to know whether the match was certainly to take place, and how soon.—Edith replied, that she had always esteemed him as a most deserving friend, and that she wished to do him every service in her power. She told

him

him the marriage was concluded on, but she could not tell the time certainly; as soon as she was informed of it, she would let him know it. He said, that was the favour he meant to ask of her; he saw that he was not despised by her, that she had generous pity for his past sufferings, and that his gratitude would not end but with his life. She said, that her friendship for him could not be shaken, unless by his misconduct, which she was persuaded could never happen. He wished for an opportunity to show his sense of her merit, and wished her to command him upon all occasions as the most humble of her servants. They repeated professions of friendship on one side, and service on the other; the time passed away unperceived, till Mabel entered the room, and the servants prepared for dinner.

Edith hoped that Clement would give them his company at table, he declared his readiness to attend her. Father Michael, the chaplain, made the fourth person at the table; they had a cheerful meal, and an agreeable conversation afterwards, till the young ladies chose to retire to their apartments, and Clement to his own.

The

The next morning, the fervant that flept in Clement's apartment told Jane, that Mafter Clement had a bleffed night, that he flept quietly, but fometimes talked in his fleep; that he talked of Madam Edith, and faid fhe had cured him. Jane charged him not to fay a word of this kind to any body but herfelf; fhe took care to convey this intelligence to the ear of her young lady, who gave her the fame injunctions.

The next day the family returned home. Sir John reproached himfelf with neglect towards his friend. Clement; he vifited him directly, and was agreeably furprifed to find him recovered of his illnefs. Lady Calverly was pleafed to hear it, they all rejoiced at it except Madam Ifabel, who took pleafure in giving him continual mortifications.

Clement defired that he might in future (when company were in the houfe) eat in the fteward's apartment; Lady Calverly imputed this requeft to his modefty, but Sir John reluctantly gave way to it.

At length the time came for this noble company to feparate. Edith kept her word to her friend; fhe told him that the marriage was not to be celebrated immediately, that Sir

C 5

Wil-

William was gone to make preparations for his approaching nuptials, and was to return at the end of a month to receive his bride; the family of Calverly were to prepare for the folemnity at that time. Clement thanked her for the intelligence; he afked permiffion of his patron to vifit fome relations at that time: he departed foon after, but not without taking a leave of Madam Edith, that was rather too tender for the ftyle of friendfhip.

The whole family were now engaged in preparing for the approaching marriage. Sir John was attentive to his fifter's intereft; he made a handfome addition to her fortune, and obtained an increafe of fettlement for her; he declared that it would be his pride and pleafure to fee all his fifters well married before he fhould engage himfelf.

Lady Calverly wifhed him to be married fooner: fhe propofed Sir Hugh Burleigh's eldeft daughter to him, he declined it refpectfully; fhe propofed the fecond and the third, but he put them by. My Lady afked, did he like any other lady better? He anfwered yes, many others. Who are they? He begged to be excufed at this time; whenever

ever he was difpofed to enter the ftate of ma-
trimony, he would certainly acquaint his
mother: this was all the anfwer Lady Calverly could get from her fon.

The month foon rolled round. Sir William Truffel returned to claim his promifed
bride. He brought with him a fifter and an
aunt to do honour to his lady, and to attend
her home to his own feat: they were efcorted
by feveral gentlemen, his relations and
friends. Sir John invited others on his part,
and the houfe was again filled with company.

Mabel's mind was engaged in the parade
and buftle of the time. She told Edith fhe
thought a wedding made a great deal of confufion and trouble in a family, and yet there
was fomething very pleafant in the preparations: that it gave a great deal of confequence to the bride, who was paid as much
refpect as if fhe was a princefs. Edith
fmiled at her remarks; fhe faid, there was
but one circumftance in it that would give
her any pleafure, and that was, being united
to the man whom fhe could prefer to all
others. " But," faid Mabel, " they fay
" one muft be in love firft; I wifh I knew

C 6 what

" what is meant by being in love ?"—" Why
" being married, to be fure," faid Urfula,
who had heard their converfation.—"What!"
faid Mabel, " muft one be married firft ?"—
" Oh yes;" faid Urfula, " people marry
" firft, and love comes afterward, for then
" it becomes a duty." — " That is very
" ftrange," faid Mabel, " I do not under-
" ftand it."—" No matter," faid Urfula,
" you will know it when it is neceffary, at
" prefent there is no occafion for you to talk
" or to think about it."—" How can I help
" it ?" faid Mabel, " when I fee and hear of
" it every day of my life."—" That is very
" true," faid Edith, " and I think Urfula
" requires too much of you, Mabel."—Urfula muttered, that " Little pitchers had
" wide ears," and many fuch good proverbs;
but Mabel could not underftand the reafon of
her prohibitions.

The nuptial rites were celebrated with all
the refpect, pomp, and feftivity, that became
the two families that day united. There
was feafting, mufic, dancing, and every ex-
preffion of mirth and happinefs.

While the company fat at dinner, an·har-
per of the Weft country came in, and performed

formed fome of his fineft airs. He fung the
noble acts of Arthur King of Britain, and
of his knights of the round table; the valiant actions of Sir Gawaine his nephew; the
ftory of Sir Triftram and the fair Ifotta; of
Sir Lancelot du Lake; Sir Lukyn, and Sir
Kaye: the treafon of the bafe Sir Mordred,
and the death of the great Arthur: the pro-
phecy of Merlin, that Arthur himfelf, or
one of his name, fhould one day reftore the
honour of Wales, and the glory of Britain,
and that this bleffing fhall long be expected
before it fhall arrive.

Madam Ifabel feemed to enjoy her own
confequence; fhe was the queen of the day,
and every one paid homage to her: healths
to her honour and happinefs were circulated
brifkly, and all the company took part in the
family joy. After dinner they retired to
dancing, and continued it till the evening
was far advanced; the bride, and her mother,
and fifters retired, and the company did not
tarry long afterwards.

The next morning early, Mabel awakened
Edith to tell her her dream. Edith chid her,
and defired her to go to fleep again. " Pray,
" my dear fifter, hear me! you cannot think
" what

" what a ftrange and curious dream I have
" had to-night." — " You never confider,
" Mabel, that you fpoil my dreams and my
" reft too; be quiet, I will not hear you."—
" Oh, my dear Edith, hear me only this one
" time! it is not a common one; let me tell
" you now left I fhould forget it."—" If
" you do I will forgive you."—" Now that
" is very crofs; it is not like my own Edith,
" but like Ifabel. I have been frightened
" very much; my heart beats fo that you
" may hear it if you liften, and I want you
" to hear and to comfort me."—" Well, if it
" gave you pain, you had better go to fleep
" and forget it."—" Yes, it gave me pain,
" that is fure, but then it gave me fome
" pleafure too. Oh, my fweet fifter, I never
" felt the like before!"—" So, then, this
" muft have been a ftrange dream; I do not
" know whether I ought to liften to it."—
" Oh, yes, you muft, indeed; I am fure
" there is no harm in it."—" Well, then,
" tell it at once, and let me hear no more of
" it."—

" Sifter, I was adreamed that I was walk-
" ing in the midft of a wood, the birds fung
" fweetly, the water murmured, the flowers
" grew

" grew round me, and the fun fhone fo bright
" that it dazzled my eyes, fo that I retired
" into the wood for to fhade me from its
" beams. So I went on and on, in a very
" narrow path, till I heard fomebody groan
" fadly, fo I went on to fee where the groans
" came from."—Here Edith laughed: " Fine
" ftuff to talk of, Mabel; I wonder you are
" not afhamed of it."—" Why fhould I be
" afhamed, Edith? You have not heard it
" yet, and I affure you it is nothing to laugh
" at."—" You muft even run on, for it is to
" no purpofe to oppofe you."—Mabel proceeded—" I went to the place from whence
" the groans came, and there I faw laid at
" his length upon the earth, the fineft young
" knight that ever my eyes beheld."—Edith
laughed again; Mabel went on—" So he
" faid he was wounded, and like to die, un-
" lefs I would cure him."—" Better and bet-
" ter," faid Edith; " I wonder where this
" dream will end!"—" So I kneeled down
" befide him; I wept for him, and I prayed
" for him, but all would not do him any
" good. He faid his enemy had wounded
" him, and his friend only could cure him.
" I afked him what I could do for him? he
" faid,

" faid, I muſt kneel down by him and kiſs
" his wounds; ſo I kneeled down, put my
" lips to his, and kiſſed him."—" Oh, fie,
" ſiſter Mabel! I proteſt you make me bluſh;
" I am aſhamed for you."—" Well, and ſo
" do I bluſh, but I do not know why,
" and yet I muſt tell you the reſt of
" it."—" Pray haſte then, to conclude."—
" I thought the knight revived by degrees;
" he aſked me to help him to riſe, I did ſo,
" and he told me I had made him well; juſt
" as Clement told you the other day."—
" So, then, you are a ſhrewd obſerver, Ma-
" bel; nothing eſcapes you."—" Well, he
" told me all his wounds were cured except
" one in his boſom, which he ſhewed me,
" but ſaid he knew a way to cure that. I
" felt ſo eaſy and happy, that I thought I
" could have flown away like a bird. I curt-
" ſied to him, and made a motion to leave
" him—he frowned and looked ſternly at me.
" I went a little way from him, on a ſudden
" he ſeized me and held me faſt; he took a
" penknife out of his boſom, he cut open
" my breaſt and took out my heart, he took
" his own heart and put it into my heart'ſ
" place, and put mine into his own boſom.
                                " I felt

" I felt fuch a pain as I cannot defcribe; I
" kneeled, wept, and prayed him to reftore
" me my heart again ; he fhewed me the
" wound in his bofom perfectly healed, but
" mine was in the fame pain as before. He
" went away from me in anger, yet ftill me-
" thought I loved him. I ftrove to follow
" him, but could not overtake him : I pray-
" ed to the bleffed Virgin and to all the
" faints in the Calendar, but none took
" pity on me. I wandered through nar-
" row paths full of briars and thorns that
" fcratched and wounded me, but ftill I
" minded nothing but the pain in my heart,
" I could even now weep to think of it."—

" Oh, my poor Mabel ! this is a fad ftory,
" indeed ; but it was only a dream, and you
" ought not to think any more of it."—
" Oh, but this is not all ! I went through a
" thoufand perils and dangers ; I was pur-
" fued by wild beafts and by venomous crea-
" tures ; I ran till all my ftrength was gone,
" and then I fell down and fainted away.
" When I opened my eyes again, I faw my
" knight coming to my affiftance ; he took
" me up and embraced me ; he faid he was
" forry to leave me in fuch a fituation, but
" that

" that he could not help it ; that my prefent
" fuffering was over, but he feared there
" was more trouble in ftore for us. He led
" me through many ugly paths, but I feared
" nothing when he was with me. At length
" we got into a better path, which opened
" upon a fine profpect : we faw a goodly
" manfion houfe, we went towards it ; as
" we came near it, we heard the found of
" mufic and rejoicing. He led me into a
" great hall where many people were toge-
" ther. They came and welcomed me as
" the miftrefs of that houfe, and faid that
" the gentleman was mafter of it. All my
" relations were there to meet me, an enter-
" tainment was prepared, I was placed under
" a canopy with my knight by my fide, and
" he called me his charming bride. I felt
" myfelf fo happy as I cannot defcribe ; I
" thought nothing of my paft fufferings, but
" that now they were well rewarded. All
" on a fudden methought the canopy fell
" down upon our heads, and crufhed us both
" to death. I ftarted, fhrieked, and awaked
" in fuch a terror as is paft all defcription.
" My poor heart beat as if it would come
" through my body, and I could hardly fetch
" my

" my breath; this made me waken you, in
" hopes you would comfort me: I afk your
" pardon for difturbing you, but really I
" could not help it."—" My dear Mabel I
" forgive you with all my heart: I am not
" furprifed that you fhould be terrified at fo
" alarming a dream, I am affected by it my-
" felf; but, indeed, my fifter, you give too
" much attention to dreams; if you were to
" endeavour to fupprefs them, and not talk
" or think of them, I verily believe you
" would not dream fo much."—

" Well, my dear Edith, I will ftrive to
" follow your advice henceforward, for truly
" I do not wifh to have any more fuch
" dreams as this laft."—" Then, my dear,
" you will make a wife ufe of it, and, per-
" haps, avoid fuch in future.

" It is time for us to rife; let us rejoice
" and be thankful for the bleffings that fur-
" round us, and not fuffer idle dreams to in-
" terrupt our happinefs."——

The young ladies arofe, they were nearly
dreft when the fervant entered the room.
Edith begged her fifter not to tell her dream
to the maid fervant, nor to talk with her
upon fuch fubjects, nor be too familiar with
her.

her. " May I not tell Urfula ? She tells me
" her's fometimes."— " You may if you
" choofe it; but believe me fhe will chide
" you for it."—" What for dreaming ?"—
" Yes, and for talking about it too."—
" Well, you are all fo much wifer than I,
" that I find I muft either keep filence or be
" corrected."---" Correct yourfelf, my dear
" Mabel, and you will want no other moni-
" tor."—Mabel fighed, " You will either
" chide me or laugh at what I am going to
" fay ; but my heart feels now as if it had
" been removed out of its place."—" Com-
" pofe yourfelf, my fifter ; have a little pa-
" tience, keep your own fecret, and all will
" come right again."—This dream made an
impreffion oñ Mabel's mind which fhe could
not foon get rid of.

The family was fummoned to breakfaft
at a later hour than ufual ; the ladies met
in the eating parlour, the gentlemen in the
great hall. The old harper was fummoned
to attend them. He fung the bleffings of
holy marriage, examples of conjugal fidelity
and happinefs, and the punifhments that fucceed the violation of the marriage vow. He
fung the chafte and noble love of the fair
prin-

princefs Eleanor to her lord Edward, the firſt
of that name ſince the conqueſt; how ſhe
ſucked the poiſon from his wound to the ex-
treme hazard of her own precious life; but
Providence inſpired the injured prince of
Joppa to vindicate his honour, and reſtore
her to her deſpairing lord. He ſung the
loves of Henry the ſecond and the fair Ro-
ſamond; the jealous rage of an incenſed
queen, and the deplorable end of that beautiful lady. A warning to princes as well as
private men. How Henry, with all his
great and kingly qualities, loſt the duty and
affection of his queen, and of his children,
by his incontinence, and was forſaken in his
old age by thoſe who ſhould have made his
latter days honourable and happy. He ſung
of the long, happy, and unſhaken union
of the illuſtrious king Edward the third, and
his excellent lady the queen Philippa; he
prayed for the proſperity of their generous off-
ſpring, and wiſhed there might never be wanting one of the race of Plantagenet to ſit
upon the throne of England.

The harper was generouſly rewarded for
his pains; he was noticed by all the company; Sir John Calverly entertained him, and

ɪ   paid

paid him the ufual fees, and the bridegroom made him an handfome prefent befide.

The gentlemen divided into parties; fome walked in the garden, fome rode out on horfeback; they all returned to dinner, where they met the ladies, and fpent the evening in dancing, or in agreeable converfation.

Mabel was ordered to fpend fome hours with Urfula, and though forewarned, fhe could not forbear telling her dream. Urfula made very ferious remarks—" It feems to " me," faid fhe, " that you will fall into " trouble from your own mifconduct, and " towards men efpecially."---" Then you do " believe in dreams after all that you have " faid againft them ?"---" No, not in every " idle fancy; but fometimes they may be " fent as warnings, to prepare us for great " events, and to put us upon guarding " againft the confequences of our faults. " Thus, for inftance, you fhould fupprefs " your love for talking, your exceffive curi- " ofity, and your freedom of behaviour to- " wards men, left fome one fhould take ad- " vantage of your imprudence, and make " you feel that pain in your heart that was

" fo

" fo grievous to you: thus you may make 'a
" wife ufe of your dreams, as well as of eve-
" ry other method of inftruction."—" Is
" love always attended with a pain in the
" heart, Urfula?"—" Yes, my child, except
" when people are fo wife as to wait for the
" commands of their parents, and accept the
" hufband they recommend; in that cafe
" they need apprehend neither pain nor trou-
" ble."—" Nor yet pleafure I fuppofe, Ur-
" fula?"—" That is a very impertinent fup-
" pofition; you fhould hear more and fpeak
" lefs; you fhould not fuffer your mind to
" run upon ftories of knights, and 'fquires,
" and fine houfes and gardens, and fuch idle
" fancies. Pray to the bleffed Virgin to af-
" fift you and to guard you againft the dan-
" gers of your fex."—" Ah, but how can I
" help it, Urfula, when I fee them every
" day before me, when the houfe is full of
" gay company, and there is feafting every
" day, and dancing every evening?"—" Well,
" that is true, I cannot deny it: thefe
" things are likely to put idle thoughts into
" young heads; however you muft ftrive
" againft them: thefe frolics will foon be
" over, the company will foon leave us, the

.2   " houfe

" houfe will be quiet again, and I fhall be very
" glad when it is."---" Ah, but, Urfula, I
" am afraid I fhall be very forry when they
" go away, and how muft I do to help it ?"---
" Mind your leffons, and your works, and
" your prayers, and they will cure all vain,
" idle thoughts and wifhes."---" Well, I
" will try all I can, Urfula."——

The company were feparated after fpend-
ing three weeks at Calverly-hall. Sir John
attended Sir William and his lady to their
own manfion, and fpent fome weeks there.
The family returned to its ufual ftate of
quietnefs and uniformity. Edith enjoyed the
tranquillity of a private life, but Mabel re-
gretted the lofs of the gay company; neither
of them grieved for the departure of their
fifter, and even the mother bore it with great
philofophy. Mabel was rather of a roman-
tic turn of mind ; the old houfekeeper had a
great collection of ftories. Mabel often vifited her apartments, and furnifhed herfelf
with fubjects for her dreams at night, and
her waking reveries.

Sir John went from his brother-in-law's
feat to London, where he fpent fome time,
and found all his former fears and doubts renewed

newed. Very foon after the Parliament broke up, the King returned to his former courfes. He quarrelled with the Duke of Glocefter; he obliged him to releafe the Earl of Suffolk, his evil counfellor; he threatened to revoke every thing done in the late Parliament, declaring againft advice, which he called compulfion. Sir John Calverly attempted to convince him of the dangers he incurred, but he held every man for his enemy that oppofed his conduct.

Clement Woodville met Sir John in London; he was quite recovered in health and fpirits, and returned with him to Calverlyhall, where he was gracioufly received by every part of the family. Sir John was very fond of his younger fifters, whofe graces and merits rofe upon him daily; he wifhed to fee them happily eftablifhed. He was commiffioned to make a propofal to Edith; it was an old knight and a widower that offered. Sir John infifted that this propofal fhould be left to his fifter's determination, and that fhe fhould not be urged, nor yet over-perfuaded to accept it. Lady Calverly mentioned it with this permiffion. Edith refufed it abfolutely, and gratefully acknowledged the li-

D berty

berty allowed her. When Lady Calverly was alone with her fon, fhe reported Edith's denial. . He faid he expected it, and was not furprifed. He faid, " My dear mother has " often wifhed me to marry; fhe has recom-" mended feveral deferving young ladies to " me. I would pay every kind of refpect to " her opinion, but the heart will make its " own choice in preference to that of any " other perfon. The truth' is, mine has " long fince fixed upon its object, and I muft " either marry to pleafe myfelf, or elfe re-" main fingle."——

" Sir John, I fhall rejoice to fee you mar-" ried, provided the lady is a fuitable match " for you. I hope you refpect the honour " of your family too much to introduce an " improper perfon into it."——

" Pray, Madam, tell me your requifites " for the wife of your fon, and then I fhall " know whether my beloved object can an-" fwer to them."——

" Firft, I expect that fhe fhall be defcend-" ed from an honourable family."——

" Very well, Madam, we can anfwer to " that point."——

" Se-

" Secondly, She fhould bring you a for-
" tune fufficient to enable you to pay your
" fifters and brothers their portions without
" making any alteration in your prefent man-
" ner of living."——

" There we muft fail : but what fhe wants
" in fortune, fhe fhall fupply in merit."——

" Merit may as eafily be found with a
" good fortune as without it, and the woman
" you make your wife will expect the fame
" expences and indulgencies if fhe brings no
" fortune, as if fhe had brought an equal
" one."——

" That may be true, Madam ; but where
" thefe requifites muft be feparated, I fhould
" choofe merit in preference to fortune. I
" will be contented to retrench my manner
" of living, to be bleft with the woman I
" love."——

" I feared fomething of this kind from
" your declining my recommendation ; I am
" concerned to find it fo. Your wife, Sir
" John, ought to have fome dignity to com-
" mand the refpect of others, to fupport and
" adorn your family and confequence."——

" She will adorn it with the dignity of
" virtue, prudence, and œconomy ; I fay no-

" thing

" thing of her beauty and accomplifhments,
" I throw them into the fcale."—

" She ought to have had a good educa-
" tion."—

" She has had the beft this country can
" afford. She loft her mother while fhe was
" an infant, her father died while fhe was
" ftill a child; her friends placed her in a
" convent, where fhe has been under the par-
" ticular care of the abbefs, who fpeaks
" highly of her merits and virtues."—

" And who is this paragon of beauty and
" accomplifhments?"

" I am not afhamed to name her, Maria
" Woodville."—

" Ah, me! all my fears are verified in
" defpite of all my precautions."—

" Your precautions were wife, but they
" were ineffectual; I thank you for your
" cares for the dear girl's education: you de-
" figned her for a nun, but fhe has no voca-
" tion to it. The abbefs is my friend, fhe
" knows of my attachment and feconds my
" views."—

" Then you muft have practifed upon her
" integrity, and you have fucceeded by fuch
" means as you will not acknowledge. To

" what

" what purpofe, Sir, do you confult me when
" you have taken your refolution and your
" meafures ?"—

" Becaufe, Madam, I wifh you to con-
" fent to my marriage; becaufe I would
" have you be a mother to my wife as well
" as to your other children, and that you
" fhould extend your advice and protection
" to her alfo: fhe reveres you, and would
" fubmit to your injunctions."—

" I cannot approve nor confent to it. Your
" father never intended that the Woodvilles
" fhould be his heirs."—

" He adopted them for his children; he
" recommended them to my care in his laft
" moments; he did not forbid me to ally
" with them; I have perfuaded myfelf
" that he would not have oppofed my
" wifhes."---

" People eafily believe what they wifh to
" be true. I am of a different opinion; but
" what will that avail if you have taken
" your refolution ?"---

" It is taken, Madam, and I am forry that
" you are difpleafed with it."---

" I have alfo taken mine, Sir; I and my
" daughters will go to Eglantine Bower,

" which

" which I referved for my retreat ; we will
" not ftay here to do honour to your
" bride."---

" I am forry for it, Madam ; nothing
" could give me fo much pleafure ; I honour
" my mother, I love my fifters, and I hoped
" that we fhould continue together, and be
" a happy and united family."---

" Sir William and Lady Truffel will be
" proud of their new relation, Sir."---

" My fifter Ifabel is too proud to be hap-
" py, or to make others fo. I thought that
" quality was of her own rearing, but I
" fear fhe derives it from you, Madam."---

" I leave you, Sir ; I can hear no more af-
" ter this reproach."---

" No, Madam, I will leave you. Con-
" fider, of what has paffed, confent to your
" fon's happinefs, and he will always con-
" fult your's."——

Sir John left his mother to her reflections ;
they were painful to her ; fhe kept them in
her own bofom, ftill hoping to vanquifh his
refolution. She made feveral attempts, but
to no purpofe. A coldnefs took place between them, and my lady made preparations
for leaving Calverly-hall.

She

She had an old fervant called Gervafe Bramber, who had lived in her father's family, and in whom fhe put confidence. She told him that Sir John was likely to be married foon, and fhe had always intended, whenever that event happened, to remove to Eglantine Bower.

She ordered him to go thither to prepare the houfe for her reception, to felect fome of the tenants' fons and daughters to be her fervants, and to have the houfe aired, and got ready as foon as poffible.

Lady Calverly's coldnefs extended to Clement Woodville, who till now had been one of her favourites : fhe began to fear that future alliances might arife ; and fhe behaved with pride and referve to him. Clement complained to his friend, who refented it for him, and this family, formerly fo happy, was now full of diftruft and fufpicion.

Sir John afked his mother whether Clement had done any thing to difoblige her, and why fhe had altered her behaviour to him.

My lady anfwered, it was high time that he fhould be kept at a greater diftance both by her and her daughters.

Sir

Sir John smiled. He told her this precaution came rather too late.

My lady was angry. " It is a mother's " duty to guard her daughters, Sir; I know " that Clement actually once looked up to " Isabel."—

" Perhaps he might, Madam; I am sure " she looked *down* upon him, and it was " hard that the poor lad might not admire " her in silence, for even her vanity should " have excused him."—

" I am answered, Sir John; my precau- " tions are justified. Perhaps you may en- " courage him to aspire to one of your sis- " ters. It is time that I should remove my " daughters from your house; I suppose " Clement knows your heart and your opi- " nions on these points."—

" Yes, he knows my heart and I know " his; but there are many things which he " is ignorant of, particularly my addresses to " his sister Maria : his elder brother knows " it, and so shall he in due time."—

" I am, indeed, surprised that you keep " any thing from him."—

" My dear mother, you may trust in " Clement's honour and prudence, and I " wish

" wiſh you would place ſome confidence in
" me."---

" Oh, my dear ſon, that you would give
" me more reaſon for it!"---

This converſation was concluded by the
entrance of the young ladies. Sir John took
Mabel upon his knee; he aſked her whether
ſhe ſhould like that he ſhould give her a
new ſiſter inſtead of Iſabel? She anſwered,
ſhe ſhould like any thing that would make
him happy. " That is my dear little girl,
" and you will love your new ſiſter dear-
" ly?"---" I ſhall love all thoſe that you do,
" as long as I live."---" I thank you, my
" ſweet ſiſter. What ſay you, my Edith?"---
" I ſay as my ſiſter does, that I will love and
" reſpect all thoſe that are dear to you,
" Sir."---" I will ſtudy to requite your af-
" fection, and ſo ſhall thoſe whom I love
" beſt, or they ſhall no longer be dear to
" me, I promiſe you."---

My lady turned the ſubject to her intended removal.

Sir John expreſſed great concern to be deprived of their company; he endeavoured to
ſoften her upon the ſubject, but ſhe was firm
and reſolved.

Sho

She told her daughters to prepare for it as foon as old Bramber fhould return, and all things were ready for their reception.

While the family were in this fituation, Clement met Edith in her favourite walk in the garden. He told her that he was juft then informed of Sir John's intended marriage. He expreffed furprife in regard to the perfon whom he fhould honour with his hand, and his concern at Lady Calverly's refolution to remove to the Bower before the wedding, which declared her difapprobation of it. He complained that he was involved in her difpleafure, though he had done nothing to deferve it. Edith comforted him, fhe defired him to bear patiently the prefent coolnefs of her mother, fhe was certain that her difpleafure would not be of long continuance; that when Sir John was actually married, fhe would relax in her feverity, and by degrees all things would come right. She knew her mother's affectionate heart would not fuffer her to be long upon ill terms with her fon, whom fhe loved and honoured; that fhe would be reconciled and make all her children happy.

" May

" May it be fo !" faid Clement, " but in
" the mean time we are deprived of your
" company; I know the value of your's,
" Madam, fo well, that not even that of my
" fifter can make me amends for it."---·

Edith bluſhed at this ſincere compliment ;
ſhe ſaid ſhe hoped they ſhould ſee each other
ſometimes, and that ſhe ſhould always remember him.

Clement was more warm in his expreſſions
of everlaſting gratitude, reſpect, honour,
and ſubmiſſion. If Lady Calverly did not
forbid him, he would certainly pay his reſpects to her at the Bower; and in caſe of a
reconciliation, he ſhould frequently find or
make occaſion for his viſits.

They parted with repeated promiſes of
eternal friendſhip.

Old Bramber returned with tidings, that
Eglantine Bower was ready to receive his
lady. Sir John had another converſation
with his mother; in addiion to all that he
had ſaid before, he warned her of the cloud
that hung over the land ; that he feared the
king and his people would go to extremities
with each other. In caſe of a civil war a
family of women might want a protector,

and

and he could not fo well difcharge that duty
as if fhe continued under his roof. Neverthelefs he would always be ready to render
her every fervice in his power, and defired
her to command him freely ; that in cafe of
danger he would fend a trufty friend, and
fome of his vaffals, to defend her upon the
firft notice. My lady was affected, fhe wept,
but her heart remained inflexible ; fhe took
an affectionate leave of him, faying, the
ftep fhe was taking was what fhe had always
refolved when he fhould marry.

Sir John fpoke to his fifter Edith, he begged her influence in his behalf, to foften his
mother, and difpofe her to a reconciliation,
and a friendly intercourfe between the two
families. Edith affured him that nothing
in her power fhould be wanting ; fhe told
him, as fhe had Clement, that fhe was certain when he fhould be married, but not before, her mother would relax ; that it was
better to let things reft as they were at prefent, and not to urge my lady any farther,
as her refolution was fixed for her departure,
and fhe had named a day in the following
week. He was convinced that fhe was right,
and determined to follow her advice.

Sir

Sir John defired his mother to take whatever fhe liked of the furniture, and fuch of
the fervants as fhe chofe to attend her. She
thanked him and named them. She defired
the old houfekeeper might go with her, and
recommended Urfula to fucceed her. She
took Beatrice her own maid fervant, and
Jane to wait on the young ladies. Old
Bramber, and young Jacob his nephew for
her footman, and fhe fhould fupply the reft
when fhe came to the Bower.

Clement offered his fervices, and begged
permiffion to attend her on her journey—
fhe wifhed him well, but refufed his attendance; fhe chofe to have none but her own
fervants to attend her.

At length the day of parting arrived.
They took a filent farewell. The young
ladies' eyes were fwelled with tears, and they
left Calverly-hall with apparent reluctance;
but my lady's firmnefs was a leffon to them
to fupprefs their emotions. She looked very
ferious, and her heart was oppreffed with
painful recollections.

They travelled in a kind of wain, with an
awning over it, not near fo well made as a
caravan of our times; they had cufhions to
fit

fit on, and their paraphernalia was with them. Another waggon carried the goods my lady had felected for herfelf. Sir John infifted on fending his fervants with them to conduct and protect them. The roads in thofe times could hardly be called by that name. A modern fine lady would have been fhaken to pieces, in her own dialect; but thefe travellers arrived whole and in good health at their Eglantine Bower. They lay two nights on the road; the firft at a vaffal's of Sir John, the fecond at a farm of my lady's, and the farmer attended them home.

Eglantine Bower had many beauties, it had alfo its defects. It was fituated in a valley between two hills. A rivulet ran near the houfe and through the garden, which had many pleafant walks in it; one particularly that was fhaded from the fun. Behind it, was a thick wood, which had a winding path up the hill, and abated the afcent to it. In the thicker parts of it there were feats here and there for reft and meditation. Through it you faw a beautiful profpect on the oppofite fide, where the afcent was more gradual; there were to be feen the fpires of churches, monafteries, and houfes interfperfed, which

was

was more pleafing to the beholder. There were cattle feeding, and the occupations of the hufbandmen all around, which enlivened the profpect and cheered the heart. The houfe was neat and convenient. The jeffamines, eglantines, and woodbines, grew round the windows, and fometimes forced their way in the rooms.

The front of the houfe faced the rifing fun, the windows were bowed, and there was a balcony in the center, that gave a full view of the agreeable profpect all around. Lady Calverly was partial to this houfe, becaufe it recalled to her mind many agreeable fcenes of the youthful part of her life. The rivulet proceeded from the branch of a neighbouring river, and fupplied the houfe with fifh of many kinds, and it afforded amufement to the patient angler.

Lady Calverly found employment for many weeks in fetting her houfe in order, and regulating her houfehold. Here we fhall leave this branch of the family for the prefent, and return to Sir John.

He reflected upon his fifter Edith's advice, and was convinced by it. He fet out for London a few days after, attended by Clement,

ment, with a refolution to conclude his marriage as foon as poffible. Richard Woodville was too well pleafed to fuffer unnecef-
fary delays; the week following Sir John
was married to his long-beloved Maria.
The wedding was kept at her brother's, who
was then courting an heirefs of great fortune, and a ward of the crown. The King
favoured his addrefs, and he was fortunate in
his purfuits both in love and ambition. Sir
John and his lady fpent a month with him
before they went to Calverly-hall.

In thofe times there was very little varia-
tion of fafhion; the fame kind of garments
continued in fafhion during the life of the
wearer. The grand fuits of clothes were
only worn upon high days, feftivals, birth-
days of the king, queen, and heir-apparent
of the crown, marriages, chriftenings, and
other great occafions. Their clothes fometimes defcended to their children, and fometimes were devifed by their wills to their
friends, favourites, and fervants, and thefe
legacies were highly valued.

When we read of the magnificence of
former times, we muft underftand them with
great limitations. It is true that they fometimes

times wore cloth of gold, but how manu-
factured we know not; the fashion of the
garments we can guess by the remains of an-
tiquity, by pictures, monuments, medals,
and coins.

Cloth of gold was often lined with wool-
len, or stuff, and not always of the finest
kinds.

He clothed his children then—not like to other men,
    In partye colours strange to see,
The right side cloth of gold—the left side to behold,
    Of woollen cloth still framed he.
Men thereat did wonder---golden fame did thunder
    This strange deed in every place.
                Ballad of the K. of France's Daughter.
            See Percy's Songs, Vol. III.

Not two centuries ago the gentry lay upon
beds stuffed with straw, and the coverings
were of coarse and ordinary materials. The
household furniture was very rudely made
up; it was sometimes covered with silk or
velvet upon great occasions, but very mean-
ly in common.

· The floors were made of clay, and when
they became so dirty that the sight of them
could not be endured, they were strewed
                                        over

over with rushes, and this was repeated as
often as there was a fresh layer of filth upon
it. This custom was the cause of many epidemical diforders in London, we may read
of them in history by the name of the plague;
but there is great reason to believe they did
not resemble the plague of the Eastern countries, but were occasioned by this and other
uncleanly customs.

Our anceftors were magnificent in some
refpects, while in others they were mean and
uncomfortable; they were ignorant of the
arts of polished manners and of refinements
in luxury.

We may with truth affert, that an ordinary citizen or tradefman in London, in the
eighteenth century, lives in a ftate of more
elegance and luxury, than men of the firft
rank and fortune did in the fourteenth, fif-
teenth, and even the fixteenth centuries;
nay, than the greater part of the fovereign
princes of Europe.

In our days it is the cuftom to complain of
poverty and oppreffion, but when we behold
the dreffes, luxuries, and manners of the
lower degrees of people, we muft either
doubt the truth of thefe affertions, or elfe
we

we muſt believe that they had rather ſee the ruin of themſelves and their poſterity, than retrench the leaſt article of their ſuperfluous expences.

In the times of our Gothic anceſtors, frugality was an eminent virtue; the man who lived, or dreſſed beyond his degree in life, would have been ſcorned, ſhunned, and deſpiſed by all his neighbourhood.

Sir John Calverly and his Lady made their appearance at court; they were gracioully received by the King, who remembered and recited the ſervices of Sir Hugh Calverly to himſelf and his family.

We do not pretend to deſcribe their dreſſes upon this occaſion, but it is preſumed they were ſuitable to their rank and fortune, and the times in which they lived; their inward habits were thoſe of virtue, honour, and fidelity.

King Richard was too fond of dreſs and gewgaws; he loved public ſhews, and every thing that indicated a light, vain, and frivolous mind.

Mr. Woodville detåined Sir John and his bride ſix weeks in London, and would have kept them ſtill longer, but they wiſhed to be

at

at Calverly-hall, and to enjoy the pure and unmixed pleafures of the country. Sir John's heart yearned after his mother and fifters; he longed for a perfect reconciliation and a conftant intercourfe of friendfhip and good offices, between himfelf and every part of his family. Such are the genuine wifhes and fentiments of an uncorrupted and affectionate heart.

As foon as they arrived at Calverly-hall, Sir John difpatched a meffenger to Eglantine Bower, with a letter to this effect:

" Sir John Calverly and his beloved wife,
" throw themfelves at the feet of their ho-
" noured and beloved mother Lady Calverly;
" they implore her bleffing, and her prayers,
" in order to complete their happinefs.

" They requeft the favour of a letter to
" convey thefe bleffings, and the congratula-
" tions of their dearly-beloved fifters, Edith
" and Mabel; and they pray daily for the
" health and happinefs of all at Eglantine
" Bower.

" JOHN and MARIA CALVERLY."

Cle-

Clement Woodville would fain have accompanied this meſſenger, but Sir John would not permit it. " Let us wait to ſee the ef-
" fect of our letter : to go now would pro-
" bably draw down an interdict upon your
" viſits in future. There will come a day
" when you will be invited to Eglantine
" Bower ; in the mean time let us leave it
" to time and affection, to ſubdue obſtinacy,
" which will deny to others what it wiſhes
" for in its own heart."—Clement ſubmit-
ted, but his heart travelled with the meſſenger and foreſtalled his reception.

My lady was diſtreſſed how to anſwer this letter; but ſhe ordered the perſon that brought it to be entertained and accommodated. She ſhowed the letter to Edith and Mabel, they were concerned in it, and ſhe conſulted them about anſwering it. This was the time for Edith to uſe her influence, which ſhe did not fail to do. " They are now actually mar-
" ried. My dear mother will not long keep
" her reſentment againſt a ſon who is an ho-
" nour to his family, and who dearly loves
" his mother and ſiſters. You will certain-
" ly be reconciled to him one time or other ;
" the ſooner you forgive, the greater will
" be

" be the obligation. My brother will visit
" us, we shall return it, and we shall be again
" a happy family. Oh, my dearest mother!
" let your Edith prevail upon you to return
" a kind and affectionate answer."—

Lady Calverly's mind was perplexed, ob-
stinacy kept its hold, but affection shook it
every hour ; her daughters urged her warm-
ly ; she chid them gently, and yet felt their
importunities.

Edith begged that she might answer the
billet ; my lady said she might ; adding, " if
" I do not like it, I need not send it."—
Edith wrote thus :——

" Lady Calverly returns the blessings,
" prayers, and good wishes of her children.
" Edith and Mabel send hearty congratula-
" tions, and affectionate wishes to Sir John
" and Lady Calverly : they all unite in
" prayers for their happiness."

My lady objected to this answer. It was
too humble and condescending to a son who
had married against her wishes and declared
disapprobation. She took up the pen herself,
and wrote as follows :——

" Lady

" Lady Calverly is doubtful whether she
" ought to answer the note that brings an
" account of her son's marriage, after ha-
" ving declared her wishes to the contrary ;
" nevertheless she cannot forget that she is
" his mother : she wishes he may find happi-
" ness in the lot he has chosen for himself.
" Edith and Mabel send congratulations and
" good wishes."

Edith begged her mother not to send the
last written : my Lady would not send the
other. A sudden thought rose in Edith's
mind ; she put her own letter into her pocket, and gave up to her mother. My Lady
sealed her's and made it ready. She desired
to know when the messenger was ready to
return ; she went out of the room—Edith
seized the opportunity ; she folded her own
note exactly like the other, she directed it
as nearly to her mother's as possible. She
substituted her own in the place, and took
the other up stairs with her, and laid it by
safely. She put on a cheerful countenance
and went into her mother's apartment ; she
took her work and pursued it. The servant
came to acquaint my Lady that the messenger

ger was ready to depart. She ordered her
to give him the letter that was laid upon the
table in the parlour. Edith blufhed and felt
fome painful emotions; fhe doubted whether
fhe had not been guilty of a fault, however
fhe did not attempt to recall it. She refolved to fay no more upon the fubjeдt left fhe
fhould betray herfelf.

The next day my Lady looked as if fhe
had not refted well; fhe revived the fubjeдt
herfelf, and Edith declined it, faying,
" What is done cannot be undone."—My
Lady fighed deeply; her daughters obferved
it. Mabel afked if fhe was well---fhe faid,
" Not quite well."—Edith expreffed concern : her mother took her hand in her's—
" Oh, my Edith ! you know me better than
" I do myfelf! that letter I fent to your
" brother !"—" What of that, my dear mo-
" ther ?"—" Oh, my child ! would I had
" never fent it ! I have reproached him
" with his marriage, in return for his kind
" and dutiful attention to me; I have
" wounded his noble, generous heart, and
" ftruck a dart into my own."—" Be com-
" forted, my dear mother; I can give you
" comfort."—" No, my child, you cannot;
" What

" what is done cannot be undone; you have
" faid truly."—" That is true, my dear lady,
" and if you will pardon me for what I have
" done, I will never wish it undone."—
" What means my Edith, she does not smile
" at my forrow?"—" Yes I do, my sweet
" mother, becaufe I can cure it."—She then
told the deception she had been guilty of;
she ran and fetched the letter, and gave it
into her mother's hand. My lady was furprifed and overjoyed.

She embraced her Edith; she called her
her beft child, her darling, her comforter:
she thanked her for what she had done, and
told her, from this time forward she should
hold her for her beft and fafeft counfellor.
Mabel took her part in the joy, and never
was there feen a happier family.

In a fhort time after, Sir John fent a letter
of thanks to his mother, with a prefent of
venifon to her, and fome ornamental gifts to
his fifters. Then was the maternal heart enlivened; then it felt the happinefs arifing
from the reconciliation with a beloved child.
The parent that defpifes and rejects this bleffing is unworthy of it.

VOL. I.   E   Lady

Lady Calverly in return sent a fine pair of bracelets of pearl to the bride; the letters were full of affection and tenderness: from this time there was a constant intercourse of friendship, and there seldom passed a week without some delightful proofs of it. Some months after the marriage, Sir John brought his Maria to visit his mother; they staid a week at the Bower, and Sir John insisted upon their returning home with them. Lady Calverly would have sent her daughters and have remained at home, but Sir John would not be denied.

They staid a month at Calverly-hall. The young lady, by her tender attention to her mother-in-law, subdued her coldness, and she became as fond of her as of the rest of her children.

The family union brought an increase of happiness to all the parties.

Mr. Clement came to the Hall while the ladies were there, and he was permitted to escort them home, and invited to visit them often.

Lady Calverly was invited some months after, to visit her daughter, Lady Truffel, and to be present at the birth of a child, which

which was daily expected. The young ladies were requested to be with their sister-in-
law, the young Lady Calverly, during her
absence. Clement and Edith spent many
happy hours together, in all the confidence
of friendship; they never suspected that the
regard they bore each other was any thing
more than that between an affectionate brother and sister.

Lady Truffel was very impertinently angry with her brother for his marriage, and
with her mother for being reconciled to it.
Lady Calverly declared that she had suffered
too much during her resentment and estrange-
ment from her son, and that nothing could
tempt her to undergo again so much pain and
self-accusation. She told her that pride was
the cause of it, and that she was determined
never more to give way to it. They had
several altercations upon the subject, but
neither party could convince the other. A
coldness took place between them, and Lady
Calverly resolved to stay no longer than
while her presence was necessary.

Lady Truffel brought her husband a daughter, to the disappointment of them both, and
they were ungrateful to God for the blessing

he

he had sent them, because it was not exactly what they had wished.

Lady Calverly left them as soon as she could be spared. She went to Calverly-hall; and from thence carried her daughters home.

Within the year from the marriage, the young Lady Calverly brought a son and heir to that respectable family, and gave joy to every part of it. The good lady-mother, and her daughters, were present at the birth and the baptism, and when they returned home, they were attended by Mr. Clement Woodville, who was fully restored to the friendship and confidence of Lady Calverly.

There were but few families that visited at Eglantine Bower; the ladies found amusement and employment in their own dwelling. Mabel was as lively as a bird in the spring; Edith had that happy complacency of mind, that makes a heaven in the bosom that possesses it, and contributes to the happiness of all around it.

Lady Calverly and her daughters assisted their vassals; they took care of their children, they fed the hungry, clothed the naked, visited the sick and afflicted, and were daily employed in acts of piety and benevolence;

and

and in confequence, were adored by their neighbours and dependents.

This is the fituation of all others the beft calculated for the difcharge of all the focial and relative duties; here all the virtues are kept in conftant exercife ; in towns and cities they languifh for want of employment, and too frequently expire.

The fummer was in its prime, the fun fhone in all his glory, when the two young ladies, attended by Clement, went to walk in the wood ; Mabel fpoke largely of it's beauties, and of the pleafure fhe found there.

Clement fhook his head—" Ah, my dear " lady, while you are admiring the beauties " of this wood, I am thinking of the dan- " gers of it; it looks like a harbour for noxi- " ous animals and reptiles, and worfe ftill, " for robbers and affaffins. My deareft la- " dies, never walk here alone, I befeech you ; " be always attended by fome trufty friend, " or at leaft by a man fervant : you are not " aware of all the dangers that wait on " youth and beauty."—

" I am convinced that you are right," faid Edith, " and I have fometimes told Ma-

E 3   " bel

" bel that fhe ventures too far into the re-
" ceffes of this wood."---

Mabel laughed at them both; fhe knew
no dangers, fhe feared none. She told them
fhe fhould not be afraid of being there alone,
and if they pleafed they might leave her
there. Edith chid her for her daring, and
faid fhe fhould endeavour to guard her againft
it.

"Come along;" faid Mabel, " I will
" fhow you a feat in an old hollow tree,
" where you may fee through the branches,
" and to the church on the hill, and hear
" the fweet birds finging all around you; it
" is fo charming that I can almoft think my-
" felf in heaven."---" My dear Mabel, how
" your imagination heightens all your plea-
" fures !"---" Well, Edith, and your's fug-
" gefts only fears and dangers; I will not
" change with you."---May your happi-
" nefs be always as pure and unmixed as at
" this hour !" faid Clement.————

They followed Mabel to the feat; the two
ladies fat down, and Clement leaned againft
the tree, and here they enjoyed in filence for
fome minutes the pleafure fhe had defcribed.

On

On a fudden they heard groans as from a
perfon in pain ; they ftarted, and Edith faid,
" Let us return, here are dangers too near
" us."---Clement faid, " Do you return and
" leave me here, fomebody is in danger and
" diftrefs, and, perhaps, I may relieve
" them."---The groans were repeated. Clement urged the ladies to return, but ftill
they tarried. He went towards the noife,
they followed at a diftance ; he made motions for them to return, but they refufed to
go.

They faw two men running away, as if to
efcape purfuit ; they faw at a much greater
diftance one man running towards them.

On a fudden Clement fprang from them,
and ran towards a place where they heard
ftill plainer the groans of the wounded man ;
they faw lying on the ground a man who
feemed expiring. Clement raifed his head
and laid it upon his knees ; he took his hand
and felt his pulfe. He bade him take heart,
for relief was at hand. Edith took the other
hand, and promifed him the rites of hofpitality. Mabel ftood like a ftatue, contem-
plating him with aftonifhment.

E 4   The

The perfon whom they had feen at a diftance now came up, and faw them employed
in recovering the wounded man.——He ex-
claimed---" Oh, my mafter !---thou deareft
" and beft of men ! what favage hand has
" ufed thee thus cruelly ?"---Clement told
him they had heard his groans, and as they
came to his affiftance, they faw two men,
who upon their approach efcaped. " Here
" is no time to lofe," faid he, " help me to
" carry your mafter to a houfe hard by,
" where he fhall be attended carefully, and
" every means ufed for his recovery."---

They tore down branches from the trees,
and made a kind of barrow, upon which they
laid the body, almoft without motion ; they
laid it down gently, and then carried it foftly between them. The young ladies went
before them ; they haftened to their mother,
and Édith told her all that had happened.
Mabel had not fpoken one word from the
moment fhe faw the wounded man. Lady
Calverly practifed the noble hofpitality of
thofe times ; fhe thought it a duty to relieve
the diftreffed, to vifit the fick, and to heal
the wounds of affliction, and of ficknefs.
She ordered her fervants to prepare a bed for
the

the ſtranger, and her houſekeeper to prepare dreſſings for his wounds: ſhe then ſet out with her daughters to meet the expected gueſts.

The motion made him revive; he opened his eyes and looked round him---the man ſaid, " God be praiſed! he is not dead; look " up, dear Sir, it is I! it is Bertram! this " gentleman and two young ladies have been " your preſervers."--- The wounded man ſighed, he raiſed his hand ſoftly to his mouth, he laid his finger upon his lips, and looked upon Bertram, he then bowed his hand to Clement, he cloſed his eyes, and ſeemed fainting again. Clement aſked, " Who is " your maſter?"--- " One of the nobleſt " knights upon earth," he anſwered. --- " His name?"---" Sir Roland."---" And his " ſirname?"---" I beg your pardon, Sir, I " am ordered to conceal it. He has power- " ful enemies without having deſerved them. " He has alſo friends among the firſt peo- " ple of this land."—" An Engliſhman?"--- " Yes, Sir, and of the nobleſt blood that " England owns."---" Well, we muſt wait " till it pleaſes him to inform us further."--- " I fear that will not be, Sir!"

Lady

Lady Calverly met them defcending the hill; fhe and her daughters accompanied them into the hall; they were obliged to lay down their burthen and reft awhile. The houfekeeper brought a cup of cordial water, of which fhe put a little into the ftranger's mouth, and finding that he fwallowed it, fhe gave him more, and by degrees the remainder.

All the fpectators were fixed in filent attention. The knight opened his eyes again, he looked around him. He kiffed his hand and bowed it to the ladies, and then to Clement. Lady Calverly defired him to wave all ceremony, and to accept of fuch affiftance as they could give him. He bowed his head and was filent. Clement motioned to carry him up ftairs, the fervants affifted them; they carried him gently up ftairs, and then lifted him off the barrow, and laid him upon the bed.

When they opened his bofom they perceived that he wore a coat of mail under his clothes, and found that his wounds were only in his arms and legs, except one in his left thigh, which feemed dangerous. They took off his cloathing, the houfekeeper

dreffed

dreffed his wounds, none of which were
deep except that in his thigh, but he was
faint with lofs of blood. They lifted him
into bed, and then left him, with Bertram
only, to repofe himfelf without difturbance.

This adventure afforded much fpeculation
to all the family.

Clement reported all that he could learn
of the fervant, and the ladies were furprifed
at the concealment. My Lady wondered
who this ftranger could be, of fo high quality
and his name concealed.

She then gave orders for his accommodation in all refpects, and commiffioned Clement to fee them executed, and to vifit the
ftranger and entertain him, till fuch time as
he was well enough to receive vifits from
herfelf and her daughters.

The ftranger had a good night, his wounds
looked favourably, and they hoped he would
foon recover.

As foon as his wounds were dreffed, Mafter Clement vifited him; he afked after his
health, and rejoiced that he was in fo good
a way ; he defired him to compofe his mind
and think of nothing but getting well.

The

The ſtranger anſwered only by ſigns, as he had done the night before.

Clement thought it very odd, but he reſolved to make him ſpeak if it was poſſible. " Sir, you are under the roof of Lady Cal- " verly, relict of the gallant Sir Hugh Cal- " verly, whoſe name, I preſume, muſt have " reached your ear."---The ſtranger made a ſign of aſſent.---" She is the mother of " Sir John Calverly; and thoſe two young " ladies, with whom I was walking in the " wood, are her daughters; they are lovely " and amiable, and proud of being your aſ- " ſiſtants."---A ſign of reſpect and grati- tude.---" Bertram, is your maſter dumb ?"--- After a pauſe---" He is under a ſolemn in- " junction of ſilence for a certain time : I " am ſure you would not urge him to break " it."---" No, certainly ; a penance, per- " haps ?"---" Yes, Sir, ſomething like it."--- " Very ſtrange !"--- " True, Sir." --- The gueſt looked at Bertram and made a ſign.--- " Sir, my maſter is truly ſenſible of the la- " dies' kindneſs and hoſpitality, and of your " nobleneſs and generoſity. He thanks you " from his ſoul ; he is concerned to give ſo " much trouble, and will remove as ſoon as " he

"he can do it with fafety."---" I beg that
" he will not think of it at prefent. Every
" one here is interefted in his favour, and I
" am entirely at his fervice."---

The knight bowed his head, he extended
his hand, Clement took it in his; the ftranger took Clement's hand between both of his,
he kiffed it, preffed it to his heart, and then
let it fall down gently.

" I will not intrude upon you any longer,
" Sir; I pray God to have you in his holy
" keeping, and to reftore your health and
" happinefs."---Clement retired bowing, and
left the room. He went to the ladies and
gave an account of his vifit. They were
furprifed at the fingular circumftances of his
fituation, and efpecially at his filence.

" I know not who or what he is, but his
" countenance is the moft interefting I ever
" beheld. I faw him undreffed laft night, I
" never beheld fo complete a form: all his
" motions are graceful, and his filence is more
" expreffive than the fpeech of moft other
" men."---" 'Tis ftrange," faid my Lady,
" that he fhould keep that fullen filence to
" thofe who have preferved his life: furely
" he might put fome confidence in them.
" He

" He muſt certainly have ſome reaſon for it,
" which, perhaps, will appear in due time."—

" It ſeems to me," ſaid Clement, " that I
" have ſeen ſomebody like him; his favour
" is familiar to me; I have ſeen a picture
" that reſembled him, but I cannot tell
" where; he is above the common race of
" men, and I am curious to know his hiſ-
" tory."—" You muſt talk with Bertram,"
ſaid my Lady, " and try to get it out of
" him."—" Oh, Madam, that will not be
" eaſy; Bertram is no common ſervant, and
" his maſter knows whom he truſts; how-
" ever, I will ſpeak to him as occaſions may
" ariſe."—

Clement offered to relieve Bertram and to
ſit up with his maſter, but he would not accept or hear of it. He offered a ſervant to
relieve him, but it was refuſed with acknowledgements. Several days paſſed in this manner, the knight grew better every day, but
nothing tranſpired.

Bertram deſired Maſter Clement to lend
him a horſe for one day; he wanted to fetch
freſh clothes and linen for his maſter, and to
inform ſome of his friends where he was,
and how circumſtanced. It was ordered directly.

rectly. Before he departed, he faid, " Sir,
" my mafter will be glad to fee you, if you
" will not urge him to fpeak."—" Can he
" hear well?"—" Yes, Sir."—" Then I will
" wait on him."——He did fo, and they had
an odd kind of converfation, which was pantomime on the one fide and fpeech on the
other.

Clement told him the ladies were defirous
to pay their refpects to him as foon as he
chofe to fee them ; he made figns that when
his fervant fhould return, he fhould think
himfelf honoured by their prefence.

Bertram returned at night, and a fervant
with him, bringing clothes and linen for his
mafter ; the fervant was admitted to his
chamber. He fell on his knees to him and
wept for his misfortune; the houfekeeper
was leaving the room when he entered and
made this report; they were fhut up together
fome time, and then the fervant returned and
Bertram remained. When Clement vifited
the ftranger the following day, Bertram told
him his mafter would rife and be feated, for
he could not bear to receive the ladies in bed.
This point was contefted, but the gueft
would

would not hear a word; he was determined on that head.

Clement made his report; the ladies' expectations were raised: in an hour after, Bertram came to aſk the favour of their company. He attended them to his maſter's room; he was ſeated in an armed chair, and his feet laid upon a ſtool. At their approach he endeavoured to riſe, but was unable. Lady Calverly chid him for the attempt. She deſired him not to put himſelf too forward, but wait with patience till the cure was completed : ſhe was glad to have the power to affiſt a perſon of merit in diſtreſs, and wiſhed him to command every kind of affiſtance that her houſe afforded. The knight expreſſed his gratitude by geſtures. Bertram paid his acknowledgements in words; he paid every kind of reſpeƈt to his maſter; he called him Sir Roland, and ſaid he was related to the firſt families in the kingdom.

"If we fail in paying Sir Roland due re-"ſpeƈt, he muſt impute it to our ignorance "of his quality," ſaid my Lady.—Clement ſaid ſomething of the ſame kind that ſeemed to give him uneaſineſs, he bowed his head and ſighed deeply. Clement ſaid, that Sir

Roger

Roger Morley, eldeſt ſon to the Lord Morley, was on a viſit to Sir John at Calverly-hall. The knight made a ſign to Bertram, he ſaid " *That* Sir Roger Morley is Sir Roland's " near kinſman."---My Lady ſaid, ſhe was glad ſhe knew that he was related to ſo noble a family. The young ladies were ſilent, the knight gazed on them attentively, he looked on Bertram. He ſaid, " Sir Roland is deep-" ly ſenſible of his obligations to thoſe " charming young ladies, who took compaſ-" ſion upon a ſtranger, and gave ſo generous " a proof of their goodneſs of heart; he " will never forget what he owes them ſo " long as life is given to him."—Edith then ſpoke, ſhe ſaid the happineſs was their's to have been at hand upon ſuch an occaſion, and deſired him not to call it an obligation.

After ſome more compliments paſſed, the ladies and Clement withdrew.

When they met at dinner, they could talk of nothing but the ſtranger knight. My Lady ſaid, " I am of your opinion, Clement; " I think I have ſeen ſomebody that he re-" ſembles ; and now I think of it, it is one " of the royal family ; nay, I believe it is " more than one, he is like Prince Lionel,
" who

" who died foon after his fecond marriage."—
" You bring to my mind, Madam, that I
" once faw a picture of the late Prince of
" Wales, the glory of old England; that
" picture was as like Sir Roland as thefe two
" hands of mine."

" Well, be that as it may, I do verily be-
" lieve he is a natural fon of one of the royal
" family, and his mother is related to the
" Lord Morley; let us keep thefe conjec-
" tures to ourfelves, he is really one of the
" handfomeft men I ever faw, and very cour-
" teous in all things but fpeaking."

After the ice was broken, the ladies called
upon their gueft every day, and as foon as he
was able, he returned their vifits. The
wound in his thigh made him lame and unable to fit on a horfe, but the others were
foon healed. A meffenger came from Calverly-hall, defiring Clement to return thither, unlefs my Lady had any wifh to detain
him. He fhowed her the letter, and afked
whether fhe had any commands for him.
She faid, " Why really I think I have. I
" wifh if Sir John can fpare you, that you
" would remain here till this ftranger leaves
" the houfe, for it is very aukward to have

" no

"no man in the family to entertain him,
"and to take leave of him when he de-
"parts."—Clement profeffed his readinefs to
ftay, and he fent the fervant with an account
of all that had happened, the adventure in the
wood, and my Lady's wifh to detain him
longer.

This proof of her confidence raifed his
fpirits, and he was the gayeft and the hap-
pieft man that ever attended upon fair ladies.

From the day that the ftranger was brought
to the Bower, Mabel feemed to affume a new
and different character; from being talkative,
fhe became filent; from being frank and
communicative, fhe was fo referved, that fhe
was afraid to open her heart, even to her beloved Edith. She fhunned company, fhe
walked alone in the covered walk in the garden, and was not pleafed to be interrupted.
Edith's eye was upon her, but fhe feared to
fay too much, and to difcover what as yet was
a fecret to herfelf. She waited till Mabel
fhould open her heart, and thought fhe could
not be filent much longer.

Mabel walked longer than ufual; Edith
went to feek her: fhe was in the covered
walk

walk mufing; Edith came near her unperceived, she heard her say, " What a pity that
" he is dumb !"—" So it is," anfwered Edith;
" and I do not remember that circumftance
" in the dream."—Mabel turned about, she
faw her fifter, and perceived that she had
heard her; she blufhed, hung down her head,
and was covered with confufion. Edith
went on---" Speak to me, Mabel; open
" your heart to me as you ufed to do :
" filence is not natural to you, and I am
" fure it muft be very painful."—" Oh, my
" fifter, have pity upon me !" faid Mabel;
she burft into tears and hid her face in Edith's
bofom.—" So I do, my love; truft in me,
" I will not betray your fecret; I know all
" that you can tell me ; be ingenuous with
" me, but guard yourfelf before others. I
" am furprifed that my mother has not ob-
" ferved the alteration in you."—" She has
" obferved it; she told me I was grown fe-
" rious and womanly, and she praifed me
" for it."—" That is fortunate for you, take
" the advantage of it : but do not indulge
" folitude and moping, it will increafe your
" diforder."—" Were you ever in this way,
" Edith ?"—" No, but I know the caufe and
" the

" the effect of it, and that it is in our own
" power to make it worfe by indulgence, or
" better by prudence and reftraint."—

" Can one help it, then ?"—" Yes, in a
" degree, if you are convinced that it is your
" duty to ftrive againft it, you will exert
" yourfelf to do it, for duty does not de-
" mand impoffibilities, and thus you will be
" cured."—

" Is it not ftrange that every circumftance
" in my dream fhould be realized ?"—" It
" is, my dear ; but let us think of it as little
" as poffible ; let us do our duty and leave
" the event to heaven."—" I will do all I
" can, but I cannot avoid thinking of it for
" my life."—" Well, let us go in, and when
" you find yourfelf uneafy from filence, I
" will indulge you, pity and comfort you."—
" I thank you, my fweet fifter, my heart
" feels lighter already from this converfa-
" tion ; I will do whatever you require of
" me."—

Edith led her into the houfe ; fhe advifed
her to take her needlework, and to be conti-
nually employed ; and above all things to be
conftant in praying to heaven for affiftance,
and not to doubt of being cured.

Many

Many courtesies were received and returned between the ladies and their guest, and
many silent conferences passed between the
knight and Mabel.

He gazed on her in a way that told her he
was struck with her charms, and when her
eye fell under his, he sighed; sometimes he
laid his hand upon his heart and then bowed
it towards her; at others he put his finger
upon his lips and then sighed, as if he lamented his obligation to be silent.

This pantomime was only acted when my
Lady was not present, but Edith sometimes
caught a sight of it; she trembled for her
sister's danger, and wished incessantly for the
stranger's departure.

The knight left his chamber; he leaned
upon Bertram, and came down stairs to dinner. He behaved with the greatest politeness
and delicacy, his gestures were so significant
and graceful, that he wanted not the aid of
language to make them understood. He sig-
nified his intention to leave the Bower soon;
his obligations for his hospitable reception,
and his regret at leaving so amiable a family.
Bertram attended and sometimes spoke, but
only when Sir Roland referred to him.

I   He

He dined with the family every day afterwards till his departure.

Mabel walked every day fome hours in the
garden; at the end of her favourite walk
there was a feat, the rofes and woodbines
were interwoven, and, affifted by the garden-
er's hand, formed an alcove of excellent
beauty and fragrance., Here fhe would fit,
when tired of walking, and meditate on her
dream, and the ftrange circumftances that
feemed to realize many parts of it. Hopes,
doubts, and fears, inceffantly invaded that
heart formerly fo peaceful and happy. One
day, as fhe was in this fituation, abforbed in
thought, the object of her meditations prefented himfelf before her. She ftarted, trembled, and arofe, intending to leave him immediately. He bowed moft courteoufly,
and waving his hand befought her not to
leave him. She curtfied low, and made a
motion to return into the houfe. He feized
both her hands, grafped them gently, gazed
earneftly on her face, till fhe blufhed and
turned afide to conceal it; he feated her, and
himfelf befide her, then lifted her hands to
his lips, and fighed deeply.

.Mabel

Mabel was in a tremor, she knew not what to do or say, an affecting silence was held for some moments; her situation grew every moment more dangerous---at last---" Pray "let me go, Sir! my mother!—my sister!--- " I cannot—dare not stay longer!"—

A voice the most tender and harmonious replied: " And will you go? Must I leave "you before you know all that my heart "feels? Oh; lady, stay, and hear me breathe "my soul upon your hand! I love you with "a passion the most ardent, sincere, and ho- "nourable."—

Mabel trembled so that she could hardly stand, she was glad to sit down to recover herself. "Holy Virgin! you speak---what "a miracle!" said Mabel.—"To you only " I speak;" the knight replied, " to all "others in this house I am silent. I put "my fate into your hands, and give you this "proof of my love, and of my honour. I "must leave this house in a few days. I "shall ever remember the kindness and hos- "pitality with which I have been entertain- "ed in it: but to you I owe another kind of "explanation: accept my vows, let me plight "my faith, and give me your's in return.

" If

" If you will deign to own me for your fer-
" vant, I will live; that charming hope fhall
" enable me to fruftrate all the fchemes of
" my enemies. There will come a day when
" I fhall come and demand you in marriage
" of your mother, till then I will wait for the
" firft bleffing of my life. Only give me an
" affurance of your favour, that I may hope
" to live for you; fay that you will be mine,
" and I will reft fecurely upon your word."—

Mabel's heart felt every word her lover uttered. She fighed, fhe wept, but could not
find words to anfwer him prefently. " You
" weep!" faid he, " Oh that I dared to
" think thofe precious drops were mine! I
" have heard that love is trueft that is wafhed
" in tears. May I hope that you will ex-
" change a lover's vows with me? Speak,
" lovely fair one; fpeak my doom; confirm
" my hope or my defpair."—

" What can I fay to you? I never before
" liftened to the language of love; I fear I
" am breaking a duty now; I am difpleafed
" with myfelf, and yet I am afraid of offend-
" ing you."—" That is fweetly faid; fear
" nothing. I afk you to break no duty,

Vol. I.   F   " only

" only to wait for me till I am in a fituation
" to afk your hand in holy marriage. You
" will not refufe me this promife, unlefs fome
" happier man"—" Oh, no, no ! I never faw
" a man that gave me one uneafy thought
" till now."—" I thank you, my charmer.
" May all your thoughts be happy ! May
" my remembrance be ever included in them
" till all my wifhes are realized, and I am
" bleffed with the name of your hufband !"—

The knight kneeled down; he vowed
eternal fidelity and love.

Mabel urged him to rife, fhe feared his
wound would be injured.

Her tendernefs appeared in fpite of all her
endeavours to conceal it.

The knight was convinced of his good
fortune; he ventured to feal his vow upon
her lips. He put a rich pair of bracelets
upon her arms; in the center of one of them
was his own picture, in the other that of a
warrior, whom he greatly refembled. He
told her it was his father, and was by him
given to his mother, and with that he gave
his heart and his fate. Time flew away too
faft for thefe lovers. The fun declined and
was

was near the horizon. Mabel heard some-
body in the garden, fhe told him they fhould
be difcovered.

He releafed her hand reluctantly. She ran
into the houfe, and up ftairs to her own
apartment. She took off the bracelets, kiffed both the pictures, put them into a private drawer, trembling all the time for fear
of interruption. Her heart was in fuch a
flutter, that fhe fat down to compofe herfelf.
She dreaded the fight of her mother and fifter; fhe feared their inquiries, their fufpicions, and for the firft time in her life ftu-
died concealment and artifice. She refolved
if they fhould perceive her emotions, to fay
fhe was fick, which, perhaps, could hardly
be called an untruth.

A few minutes after Mabel left the garden,
Edith entered it. She expected to find her
fifter there, and was difappointed. She went
into the covered walk, and faw Sir Roland
fitting in the alcove. He rofe at her approach, and by his geftures invited her to
fit down by him.

Edith thought fhe had never feen him look
fo handfome; there was a fire in his eyes

F 2   that

that was unufual, his cheeks were adorned
with a beautiful colour, which had generally
the pale hue of ficknefs. He looked cheerful and animated. A fufpicion arofe in
Edith's mind; fhe thought her fifter was
not far off, fhe expected to fee her every moment; fhe waited till the fun was fetting;
but fhe came not: fhe told Sir Roland that
the damps of the evening were not good for
an invalid, fhe invited him to walk into the
houfe; he led her into the hall, and fhe went
to her mother's apartment.

She inquired where was Mabel—my Lady
faid, fhe believed in her own apartment.
Edith went thither and found her fitting by
a table, with her cheek leaning upon her
hand. Edith told her fhe had been feeking
her every where, and chid her for indulging
folitude and mufing.

Mabel complained of being unwell, but
could not tell very well what ailed her.
While they were talking, the bell fummoned
them to fupper. The knight excufed himfelf by Bertram, and fupped in his own apartment. Clement began to think he was well
enough to depart. Edith feconded him.

I

My

My Lady faid it was impoffible to hint any thing of that kind, fhe doubted not that he would go as foon as he found himfelf able to travel. Clement obferved that Bertram had often been going and coming back within the laft week. Lady Calverly faid, that looked like making preparations for their departure, and it proved fo.

A few days after, Bertram declared his mafter's refolution to depart on the morrow. He expatiated upon his obligations to Lady Calverly and all her family ; he hoped there would come a time when he fhould acknowledge them more fully, and claim a continuance of her friendfhip. At prefent he muft obey the circumftances of his peculiar fituation ; that he fhould go with the deepeft fenfe of her noblenefs and hofpitality, and fhould daily remember all the family in his prayers to heaven.

My Lady returned a fuitable anfwer. Many compliments were fent and returned by all the parties concerned.

The knight dined and fupped with the family. Mabel and he dared not exchange

looks;

looks; they were upon their guard before those who observed them.

The next morning as the family was sitting at breakfast they heard the found of a horn, and presently after a number of horfemen came into the court-yard. They ranged themfelves on each fide, and a man in green blew his horn loudly. The knight and Bertram defcended the ftairs, they entered the parlour where the ladies were fitting, Sir Roland approached Lady Calverly, he took her hand and kiffed it, he bowed low and retreated; he embraced Mr. Woodville, and made figns of gratitude and friendfhip; he then laid his right hand upon his heart and bowed to the young ladies. He retired backwards, bowing till he was again in the hall. Bertram affifted him to mount his horfe, which was caparifoned with a lambfkin, the wool outward, for his eafe and convenience. He rode in the midft of the horfemen, who attended him with the utmoft refpect and deference. The man in green blew his horn and led the way, the reft followed; Bertram went laft. He gave the fervant fome notes to deliver when he fhould

be

be gone out of fight, he then gallopped after his companions.

Mabel could not meet the eyes of her mother and fifter, fhe retreated to her own apartment. She faw a letter upon her table directed to herfelf; fhe opened it and read the contents :.

" The contracted bride of a filent man
" muft learn to practife fecrecy. The huf-
" band prefumes to remind his beloved, dear
" lady, and to recommend himfelf to her
" prayers by the name of Sir Roger de Cla-
" rendon, which is his proper appellation.
" He relies upon her truth and honour, and
" bids her do the fame by him in full truft
" and confidence. He will inform her of
" his health and fafety, and reluctantly bids
" his Mabel farewell : farewell, dear lady.
                                    " R. C."

Mabel was comforted by this billet; fhe made hafte to depofit it fafely in the drawer with her bracelets, and when Edith entered the room, fhe found her more compofed than fhe expected.

Edith

Edith aſſumed a cheerful appearance; ſhe informed her ſiſter that their gueſt had left a note for her mother, and another for Clement. In the firſt he acknowledged his obligations to her, and referred to a future day, when he ſhould recommend himſelf to her favour and friendſhip. In that to Clement he apologized for his ſilence, which one of his beſt friends had enjoined, during the time of his concealment, in order to evade all inquiries, whether of danger or curioſity. That as ſoon as he ſhould find himſelf in ſafety, he ſhould write to him and claim his friendſhip. He acknowledged himſelf bound by the ſtrongeſt ties of gratitude and affection, and hoped to give better proofs than words hereafter.

He deſired Mr. Clement to preſent his acknowledgements to thoſe two charming young ladies, whoſe beauty and merits were engraved upon his heart in ſtrong and laſting characters, and he would pray for all and every part of that dear and honourable family of Calverly.

Edith told her likewiſe that he had made a handſome preſent to the houſekeeper for

her

her attendance on him in his ſickneſs, and that Bertram had given money to the men ſervants; in ſhort, that he had ſhown himſelf a moſt generous and accompliſhed knight.

Mabel expreſſed her ſatisfaction, and ſaid ſhe never doubted that he would acquit himſelf honourably upon all occaſions.

"And now, my dear ſiſter, I hope you "will renew your ſpirits and cheerfulneſs, "and reſtore my Mabel to me, as ſhe was, "before this ſtranger came hither."—"I "cannot promiſe that, my ſiſter; but I will "attend to your advice, and endeavour to "profit by it."—

"Ah, my dear! has then this man car-"ried away your heart with him as you "dreamed he did?"—"I cannot deny it to "you, Edith; he is the man that I muſt "marry, or I will die a maid."—

"And has he left his heart with you, "Mabel?"—"That I ſhall not reply to; "time will ſhow."—"Oh, Mabel, I fear "for you!"—"You need not, I do not fear "for myſelf."—"Take heed of the pain in "your heart, Mabel!"—"Take care of

F 5 "your

" your own, my fifter; I know who reigns
" there, as well, and, perhaps, better 'than
" yourfelf."—Edith blufhed. " You fur-
" prife me, fifter."—" Well, let us excufe
" each other, I will not fuffer you to be
" angry with me."—She embraced Edith.
" I will be very good, I will mind what
" you fay, my Edith; but, indeed, my heart
" feels lighter than it has done for many
" weeks paft."—" I am very glad to hear it,
" I am rejoiced to fee you fo cheerful. Let
" us go to my mother's apartment."—

The young ladies went arm in arm to my
lady, they took their work. My Lady was
full of the praifes of the knight, and of curiofity to be further informed of his family
and fortunes. Mabel appeared eafy and
cheerful, fhe was more guarded than formerly, but not lefs agreeable. The beauties of
her perfon unfolded daily, her manners improved, love taught her difcretion, her confidence in the object gave her eafe and cheerfulnefs, fhe appeared every thing that a fond
mother could wifh her to be.

When they met at dinner, Clement propofed to return to Calverly-hall; he wifhed

to

to go, before Sir Roger Morley should have left it. The knight had acknowledged him for his kinsman, perhaps he might learn some particulars from him. My Lady approved his proposal, she wished him to make inquiries, and to let her know the result of them.

He left the Bower a few days after Sir Roland, and the young ladies confessed to each other that they were very dull without them.

A servant of Lady Calverly's had married a cottager who lived within a mile from the Bower, the young ladies used to walk thither often.

Ralph and Susan Hobson were much benefited by their neighbourhood to Eglantine Bower. Lady Calverly sent them a bed, and several kinds of furniture. When Susan was with child, the young ladies made her baby clothes; they stood godmothers for their first-born, and they were delighted to amuse the child, and to work for it. Susan was happy to see the ladies coming through the fields to her cottage. She used to set the best of her fruit aside for them, a dish of scalded apples and

cream

cream was an agreeable repaſt after their
walk, and was as well reliſhed by them,
as preſerved fruits and iced creams are in
theſe days. They enjoyed the bleſſings of
nature, and knew not the adulteries of art.
An ewe died in yeaning, the lamb was brought
up in the houſe and fed by the hand, this
was deſtined to Madam Edith by Suſan, and
ſhe was with ſome difficulty prevailed on to
accept it. Mabel took pleaſure in feeding
and careſſing it, to her Edith transferred it,
and ſhe loved it the more for her ſake. It
uſed to follow them to Hobſon's cottage, and
this ſimple circumſtance contributed to the
amuſement of both the charming ſiſters.

Days and weeks rolled over their heads
without producing any event out of the common incidents of private life. Clement informed them of his brother's marriage, and
that the King had conferred the honour of
knighthood upon him. In the days of Edward the Third this was a real honour; in
Richard's time it degenerated: but it never
became venal and contemptible, till it was
made hereditary.

The

The following Chriſtmas Lady Calverly
and her daughters were invited to ſpend
ſome time with Sir John and his lady at the
Hall; Clement was ſent to eſcort them thither. My Lady would fain have made ex-
cuſes, but no denial would now be accepted.
They found company there as uſual, and reluctantly mixed in the buſtle of it. Among
the young gentlemen there was Sir Oliver
Marney, who had been there before when
Lady Calverly and her daughters were preſent. This gentleman had ſeen Edith, he
had ſighed in ſecret for her, but being under
age, and wholly dependent on his father, he
had admired her in ſilence.

By the death of a diſtant relation, he came
to poſſeſs an handſome fortune; he now pro-
feſſed himſelf her ſervant. He beſought
Sir John's influence and recommendation to
the young lady, and to her mother. He was
permitted to declare himſelf to the fair lady
a few days after her arrival at the Hall. She
received his propoſal with courteſy, ſhe expreſſed a ſenſe of gratitude for the honour he
intended her, but declined his offer. She
ſaid that ſhe choſe to remain with her mother,

ther, and would not liften to any propofal of marriage. The lover was grieved and mortified; he appealed to her mother and brother, they fpoke in his behalf. Edith was cool, but refolute. Her mother was urgent, but ftill fhe infifted upon her right to her negative.

Sir John tried his influence, but ftill fhe was fteady in her refufal. He infifted, Sir Oliver was young, he was good and amiable, he had every requifite that a lady could demand, what could be the reafon of her pofitive refufal? Edith kept her ground, fhe preferred her prefent fituation, in which fhe was happy, to any contingency. Sir John afked her if fhe preferred any other man, faying, that no young lady was likely to refufe fuch an offer, unlefs fhe had a fecret partiality for another man. Edith was diftreffed, fhe evaded the queftion, fhe begged to be allowed her negative. Sir John would not urge her further, he only wifhed to promote her happinefs, and fhe was certainly the beft judge of what would eftablifh it. Lady Calverly dreaded having Edith torn from her,

fhe

fhe was gratified by her wifh to remain with her, and fhe readily indulged it.

Sir John afked Mabel if fhe would refufe fuch an offer :—" Yes, truly," anfwered Mabel ; " I do not intend to marry for ten " years to come."—

Sir John laughed at her reply, and anfwered for his fifter Mabel, that fhe would not be unmarried ten years hence.

Edith received a note from Clement, requefting her to meet him in the garden as early as was convenient to her. She refolved to obey the fummons. She was there as foon as it was perfectly day-light, but he was there before her. He met her with trembling limbs and faultering accents.

She afked if he was fick, or what was the caufe of his agitations.

" Oh, Madam, pardon my prefumption ! " my folly ! my diftraction !"—

" What is the matter, my friend ? be " compofed and tell me."—" Only anfwer " me one queftion, Madam ; my fate de- " pends upon it."—" Speak it, Sir."—" Are " you going to be married ? Is it to Sir Oli- " ver Marney ?"—

" No,

"No, I am not; I have given a positive
"refusal."—"Thank God for that blessed
"news! I ask your pardon, but I could not
"bear the suspense; I have not been in bed
"to-night—I am half distracted---but I can
"hear only truth from those lips; you can-
"not deceive me."—"No, Clement; nor
"can I any longer deceive myself. You
"have opened my eyes, I wish you had not;
"for you have obliged me to alter my beha-
"viour, and converse with you with more
"reserve than I have hitherto done."—
"Pardon my temerity, consider the occasion.
"How could I bear the thought of losing
"you for ever?"—"Softly, my friend;
"do you remember that in this house you
"made me the confident of your passion for
"my sister Isabel?"—"Oh, me! I was mista-
"ken; I never loved her as I do you. I
"knew not then your adorable qualities; I
"admired beauty only; but now it is vir-
"tue in a human form. My passion for you
"is in my soul, it is my existence. Treat
"me as you will, I can never love you less.
"I live upon your idea when you are absent;
"I see you where you are not present, and
                                    "when

"when I am forbidden to cherish this paf-
"fion, I shall no longer wish to live."—

"Be more compofed, or I leave you. Re-
"flect upon my fituation, reduce your affec-
"tion within the bounds of friendship, and
"within thofe limits there is nothing I will
"deny you; what farther can you afk of
"me?"—

"Oh, nothing! I can afk nothing more!
"Alas, I thought it was only friendship
"that I had for you! but this potent rival
"has convinced me that it is more."—"Say
"no more, my friend; we muft fubmit to
"the reftraints of duty and of reafon: you
"muft be more cautious than ever in your
"behaviour to me. A rival's eyes are upon
"you; be prudent for my fake, if not for
"your own. I would not for any thing
"that any fufpicion of our attachment—I
"mean of your attachment, fhould arife at
"this time, there is nothing I dread fo
"much: let me affure you of my fincere
"and conftant friendship, and let that make
"your mind eafy."—

"But are you fure you fhall not be pre-
"vailed upon?"—"Yes, very certain; my
"mo-

" mother and brother have given over urging.
" me; it is all given up."—

" Heaven bless you, my dear lady! you
" have quieted a heart that was breaking; it
" is your's to preserve or to destroy it. I
" will obey you implicitly: I will be as
" cautious as you can wish; so long as you
" know the secret of my heart, and do not
" disdain its homage, I am easy."—

" Let us then change the subject. Have
" you gained any intelligence concerning Sir
" Roland?"— " No; I asked Sir Roger
" Morley many questions, he seemed re-
" served in his answers. He acknowledged
" that he had such a relation, but would not
" tell me any particulars of him."—" Well,
" make use of every opportunity to learn
" more of him, I have a foreboding that we
" shall see him again, and be acquainted with
" him."—

" Have you? Perhaps I may find another
" rival in him."—" Be silent on that subject,
" you are contending with shadows; after
" what I have said, you ought to be satisfied;
" if you are not, you will hinder me from
" putting confidence in you as I am inclined.
" to

" to do."—" Pardon me, and I will be all
" that you wish me; I will be silent, and
" submit to your commands."—" Do so,
" and you shall have nothing to complain
" of. It is time for us to separate, we may
" be observed. Farewell; be prudent, and
" be happy."——

He just touched her hand, he bowed low
and retired. Edith hastened into the house,
and up to her own apartment, where she
found Mabel risen from her bed and dressing.
She made some excuses for going down stairs,
and both ladies prepared to meet the family
at breakfast.

It was the young Lady Calverly that had
informed her brother of the proposal of marriage to Edith. He was struck with sur-
prise and vexation, and left her presence to
conceal his confusion. Within a week he
recovered his peace and cheerfulness, which
was owing to the conference with Edith.
His sister observed his dejection at the first
information, and his recovery after the denial; she laid together these circumstances,
and drew certain inferences, which she kept
in her own heart till it should be a proper
time

time to declare them. She was at this time confined to her own apartment, she was very big with child, and otherwife much indif-pofed, and was excufed from prefiding at the table.

Lady Calverly had ftaid a fortnight at the Hall, which was the time she propofed, and fpoke of her return home the following week. Sir John urged her to ftay till his Maria fhould be brought to bed, she having need of her company and advice. The young ladies wifhed to be allowed to return home, they were urged to ftay alfo. Edith faid, she found Sir Oliver Marney intended to ftay fome time longer, that his looks re-proached her, and he took every opportunity of perfecuting her with his addreffes, and she wifhed to efcape from his company.

Sir John called her a cruel girl, yet he would not detain her againft her inclination: Mabel wifhed to return with her fifter, she began to be uneafy, and did not expect to hear from Sir Roland till she fhould be again at the Bower. The young ladies refolved to return home at the time their mother had firft propofed.

Mr.

Mr. Clement Woodville begged leave to attend them. Edith made objections to it. Sir John afked for better reafons : Edith faid, that as their mother was not with them, fhe chofe to have no gentlemen attendants. The lady dowager commended her prudence, and Clement was obliged to fubmit, though he fecretly murmured at Edith's cruelty.

He was not, however, difpleafed at her leaving Sir Oliver at the Hall, for his fear was that he fhould have attended her to the Bower. Some of Sir John's fervants went home with the young ladies, and only one man and their own maid fervant befide.

They were both pleafed to return to the Bower. Mabel's heart felt lighter and happier than at the Hall. Here fhe firft faw her lover, and here fhe hoped to hear tidings of him. Mabel had a clofet appropriated to her ufe, and in it a cheft of drawers of her own : here fhe depofited her treafures of every kind ; here fhe put the bracelets, the precious pledge of her lover's vow, and his firft letter : once at leaft every day fhe took them out, kiffed both the pictures, and fome-times talked to them as if they underftood

her.

her. She found infinite pleasure in these secret visits, and always returned more cheerful, and assured of her lover's truth and honour.

A few days after her return home, the two sisters went to Hobson's cottage to see their god-child. Susan rejoiced at their return home, and set before them some winter fruit well preserved.

While Edith was nursing the child, Susan made a sign to Mabel that she wished to speak with her alone. She motioned to go into the orchard : Mabel's heart leaped at the hint ; she anticipated the business. She followed Susan, and as soon as they were out of sight, she gave her a letter, which she said was given her by a fine gentleman, who looked like a lord, and behaved with so much graciousness that she could not refuse him. Mabel snatched the letter, she bade Susan go into the house, and hold her sister in talk till she came in. She opened it hastily with trembling eagerness, and read the contents:

" God

"God blefs and preferve you, my deareft "lady! I have the pleafure to inform you "that I am recovered of my lamenefs, and "reftored to perfect health. I labour in- "ceffantly to eftablifh my fortunes. My "enemies are among thofe neareft to the "King; neverthelefs, I do not defpair of "obtaining his protection as foon as I can "gain admittance to his prefence, for he "knows me well.

"I have lamented your abfence from the "Bower, but you are returned and bring "peace to my heart. I am told you go of- "ten to goodman Hobfon's, whofe wife was "your fervant. This gives me hopes of one "day feeing you there: do not refufe to "meet the man whofe health and happinefs "are in your keeping. I am your's living "or dying."

"R. DE CLARENDON."

Mabel was enlivened and comforted by this intelligence; fhe went into the houfe and took her fhare of nurfing, till Edith motioned to return home.

She

She went up to her clofet and paid her daily homage to her pictures; fhe read over her letter, one paffage ftruck her—" My " enemies are thofe neareft the King; but I " do not defpair of his protection as foon as I " can gain admittance to his prefence, for he " knows me well."

" How can this be? Why do they keep " the King from feeing him? If the King " knows and loves him, why does he fuffer " it? Who is this man, then? Is he related " to the King? Is it the intereft of his " enemies to prevent his feeing him? Per- " haps fo."——Mabel uttered thefe words over the letter in her hand. She laid it down; fhe took up the pictures; fhe look- ed at that of Sir Roland's father. " Holy " Virgin! what do I fee? Edward Prince " of Wales, A. D. 1347. Good heaven! " he was then my knight's father! he is the " King's brother, and his enemies are among " the King's relations! I underftand all that " he has faid in this letter."—She fell into a profound reverie, and was abforbed in it for fome minutes: fhe was awakened by Edith's tapping at the door. Mabel made hafte to

shut

shut her drawer before she opened the door. "Why do you shut yourself up here, my "dear sister?"—"Because I come here to "meditate; I was lost in thought when you "came."—"I hope the subject of your "thoughts is an agreeable one."—"Very "much so, sister."—"I am glad of it; I "feared that musing might make you me- "lancholy, and I came to seek your compa- "ny."—"I thank you, my dear Edith, I "will attend you; but I can assure you that "I am very well and very happy."—They went to their mother's apartment, where they sat down to work: Mabel was as gay as a lark, and Edith knew not how to account for the variations in her humour.

Mabel frequently walked to Hobson's cottage, generally with her sister, but sometimes with only a maid servant. Edith wished her not to go alone, as she sometimes threatened; she warned her of the dangers young women incur by walking alone, and intreated her never to walk without an attendant.

Mabel was frequently absent and abstracted; she was not pleased to be told of it, and generally made reprisals. One instance of

this happened when Edith had been obferving
her fome time, fhe ftarted and fighed.
" Where have you been, Mabel ?"--" Not far
" from home, fifter."—" In the wood or in
" the garden ?"—" Neither; I was in the
" houfe, and was thinking that we were very
" dull alone. I think, Edith, that you were
" very cruel in forbidding Clement to come
" home with us."—" I thought it would not
" look right in our mother's abfence."—
" Oh, then, you punifhed yourfelf and me
" for the look of it ?"—" What do you
" mean, Mabel ?"—" Why that I like his
" company, and I had a notion you did, but
" fuppofe I am miftaken."—" You talk very
" oddly, I do not underftand you."—" Why
" then you are an innocent, dear creature,
" and play the tyrant without knowing it."—
" Take heed, Mabel, thefe floats may one
" day come home to yourfelf."—" Then I
" will be merry while I may, and fad when
" I cannot help it."—

" Be merry and wife, however, Mabel, and
" do not allow yourfelf to jeft too much
" with thofe who love you beft."—" Who
" elfe can I jeft with ? I have nobody but
" you

"you to fpeak to. Come, I know we love
" each other, and underftand each other
" too: I wifh my knight and your 'fquire
" were here to entertain us; and that without
" a jeft or falfehood."—

" I do not wifh for either; I had rather
" my dear mother was with us; you would
" not talk in this way before her."—" Perhaps
" not, fifter; but then I fhould think the
" more, and nobody could hinder that, you
" know."—

" Perhaps our mother might convince
" you, that you ought not to let your
" thoughts run riot any more than your
" words; that it is a duty to keep them
" within the bounds that religion and virtue
" prefcribe. A mother might do this, I am
" only a fifter, but then I am a true friend,
" and might hope that my advice would
" have fome weight with you."—

" You are fo very ferious that I muft have
" done."—Mabel went and walked in the
garden for fome time, and when fhe came
back, fhe was filent and fullen, and appeared
difpleafed with her fifter's admonition.

Mabel went to Hobfon's oftener than
ever: her fifter reproved her for going with-

out

out her, and without letting her know when
she went thither. Infenfibly a coldnefs
arofe between thefe two amiable fifters, without any abatement of affection to each other,
but a ftronger magnetifm caufed for a time
a referve, and a want of confidence in each
other.

Mabel rofe early in the morning, fhe
walked to Hobfon's, found a letter there,
and came home by her fifter's breakfaft hour;
as foon as that was over, fhe retired to her
clofet and read her letter over and over.

"My dear Lady,

"I muft fhortly take a journey of great
"confequence, but I cannot go till I have
"feen you. I long impatiently for that
"pleafure, I have to fay what cannot be
"written. I will be at Hobfon's cottage
"any day that you fhall appoint, and I beg
"and befeech you to meet me there. I will
"fpeak to the good woman, and fhe will ac-
"quaint me with your pleafure.

"Your true and faithful fervant ever,

"R. C."

Ma-

Mabel's heart refigned itfelf to the direction of her lover; difcretion was filenced, advice was rejected, fhe believed that it was her fate to marry Sir Roger, and, therefore, there could be nothing wrong in obeying it.

Love is a dangerous fophifter, he excufes every thing, and feems to fanctify every thing that he enjoins. Reafon is called an intruder, and is expelled the council, and love becomes the tyrant of the heart.

The next morning Mabel went to Hobfon's and returned to breakfaft.

Edith told her fhe went thither very often. She replied, " I go as often as I pleafe, " you have no right to forbid me."—" I am " forry you fhould think me impertinent, " my fifter, I only wifh to know why you " do not accept my company, and why you " make a fecret of your walks to me."—

" Perhaps I may have reafons for what I " do; but I do not like to be called to ac-" count. You have not taken Urfula's " place, I hope?"—" Ah, my fifter! you " are unkind, I have not deferved fuch re-" flections."---" Why, then, do you extort

G 3   " them

" them from me ? Little Ellen has been very
" ill, she is cutting teeth, her mother says;
" I am anxious about her, and wish to see
" her often: sure there is no harm in that,
" sister ?"---" I am answered, sister Mabel;
" only take care that in deceiving me you do
" not deceive yourself."---" What do you
" mean ?"---" I mean that I am in fear that
" you have some concealed reason for going
" so often to Hobson's cottage."---Mabel
was confused, she affected anger to hide it,
and left her sister in displeasure. Edith was
uneasy, she meditated whether she should not
send a messenger to Calverly-hall to desire
her mother to hasten home. She suspected
that something wrong was going forward,
yet she was unwilling to give her mother
cause to suspect Mabel; she hoped she would
not be guilty of any capital indiscretion.

Several days passed away in these reflections without Edith's taking any resolution.
One morning when she went to breakfast,
Mabel was missing. Edith waited an hour, yet
she came not. " Perhaps she will not re-
" turn till dinner time."---The dinner hour
came, but Mabel came not with it. Edith
sup-

fuppofed fhe tarried to fhow that fhe would not be controuled. " Yet how greatly was " fhe altered in her difpofition and con- " duct !"---

Night came on; but no Mabel. " She is " very perverfe and obftinate, yet I will not " folicit her to come home," faid Edith ; " I " will go myfelf in the morning and fetch her " home, and I will reprove her fharply."---

The next morning it rained hard and Edith was obliged to ftay at home. She expected her every hour and minute, but fhe came not. In the afternoon fhe fent a fervant with a horfe, and orders that he fhould not come without her. In lefs than an hour he return- ed. He told her that fhe was not at Hob- fon's, that fhe went away the day before with two gentlemen, attended by feveral fer- vants.

Edith was furprifed and diftreffed; fhe then fent for the houfekeeper and confulted her ; till now fhe had kept her thoughts in her own bofom, but now fhe revealed her fears and her grief. What was to be done ? Should fhe fend a fpecial meffenger, to her mother directly, or fhould fhe wait till the

next

next morning? While they were in confultation, a letter was brought in, the meffenger would not wait an anfwer, but rode off at full fpeed. Edith read the contents:

"Mabel is fafe and well. She begs her
"dear fifter to be eafy and compofed, and
"not to alarm her mother. She will be at
"home to-morrow without fail."

"What fhall I do, Alice?" faid Edith.—
"In my poor opinion, Madam, it will be
"better not to fend to my Lady; it will
"make her unhappy, and, perhaps, do no
"good. If Madam Mabel fhould come
"home to-morrow, fhe will, I hope, give
"good reafons for her abfence; and if fhe
"fhould not, it will be time enough then
"to fend for my Lady."---"I believe you
"are right," faid Edith; "I will wait to
"fee what to-morrow will produce."---

Edith fpent an unhappy day, and reftlefs
night; fhe feared and hoped by turns; but
her greateft fear was to give pain to her mother's heart. On the morrow about noon
fhe heard a horn blow, feveral horfemen entered

tered the court, Mabel was in the midſt of them, and Bertram, Sir Roland's 'ſquire, rode by her ſide. The ſervants ran into the court-yard, Edith ſtood at the hall-door. Mabel alighted with Bertram's aſſiſtance: ſhe ran into her ſiſter's arms. Bertram bowed to both the ladies, and before Edith could queſtion him, he and his companions rode off, and were ſoon out of ſight.

Mabel held her ſiſter's hand, and led her into the dining parlour. " Forgive me, my " dear Edith, for the pain I have given " you."---Edith looked very ſerious. " Let " me firſt know whether I ought to forgive " you."---" Yes, my ſiſter, you muſt for- " give me ; and you muſt farther oblige me, " by avoiding to queſtion me on the cauſe of " my abſence. One day you ſhall know all, " but at preſent I cannot tell you ; only one " thing believe, that I have been in honour- " able company, and that I am ſafely return- " ed home to you. I was ſolicited to ſtay " where I was, and never to return hither, " but I could not conſent, becauſe it would " grieve my dear mother and ſiſter."---

" Oh, Mabel! you have given me pain, " more than you can imagine; I have not

G 5 " yet

" yet let my mother know of your elope-
" ment, but I am fearful that I shall not dif-
" charge my duty to her if I conceal it."---
" Yes, you will; I entreat you to conceal it,
" for some time, at least. I hope I shall one
" day tell it myself and be forgiven for
" it."---Edith was serious and sorrowful;
but Mabel, by her careffes and perfuasions,
foothed her into forgivenefs. She begged
her to enjoin the fame fecrecy to all the fervants; she promised not to give her the fame
caufe of complaint in future.

Edith afked many queftions, but Mabel
evaded or declined anfwering them, and
though not fatisfied, she defifted from her
inquiries.

From the time of her return, Mabel never
went to Hobfon's without inviting Edith to
walk with her. Edith queftioned Sufan,
but could get no intelligence from her. Mabel affumed a cheerfulnefs, and Edith was
obliged to keep her uneafinefs in her own
bofom.

A fhort time after Mabel's return, Mr.
Clement Woodville came to pay the ladies a
vifit. He brought the welcome tidings that
his.

his fifter, the young Lady Calverly, was fafely brought to bed of a fecond fon, and that their mother would return home in a few weeks.

Both the fifters were rejoiced at his arrival, but he thought Edith was uncommonly ferious and referved; he told her fo, but fhe denied it.

He told her all his thoughts and views: that he was offered an employment in the King's houfehold, but it was not much to his liking. That there was talk of the King's going to Ireland, and he was advifed to make intereft for a company in the army, that he liked that much better, but would be glad of her advice, and would be governed by it.

Edith declined giving advice—Clement urged it---had fhe not acknowledged herfelf his friend, would fhe refufe the duties of that office ?---She faid, fhe wifhed him to do what was moft for his advantage. He was not fatisfied with fo cold an anfwer. " Why, " then, do what is moft agreeable to your- " felf."---" Would to God I might," was his anfwer.---" What, then, would you do, " Clement ?"---" I would live to the com-

G 6　　　　　　　" forts

" forts of life, and not to the vanities or the
" luxuries of it. I would live upon a small
" eftate, and reap the produce of it; I
" would farm my own lands, grow my own
" corn, fee my cattle feed around me, and
" enjoy the bleffings of a rural life. Had I
" the power to choofe my fituation, this,
" and one dear companion by my fide, would
" be all that is wanting to complete my hap-
" pinefs. Yet for that dear friend's fake, I
" could be content to encounter dangers and
" difficulties of every kind; and there is no-
" thing I would decline for her fake : it is
" fhe that muft decide my fate, and tell me
" what courfe I muft take."---

Edith was affected, fhe was loth to give
pain to the honeft heart that refigned itfelf
entirely to her difpofal. " My friend," faid
fhe, " I will not affect to mifunderftand
" you. My firft wifh is to make my dear
" mother's life happy ; my fecond, to make
" you fo. I know your worthy heart, and
" I truft it. You muft wait with patience
" till thofe two objects can be united. I
" confefs that I wifh you to have fome em-
" ployment at home, rather than to encoun-

" ter

" ter dangers abroad; my mother loves· and
" trufts you, perhaps fhe may have occafion
" for your fervices, fhe may be under obli-
" gations to you, and·fhe may wifh to re-
" ward your attachment. to her. This·is
" my plan, and this is all that I. can offer
" you."—" And this fhall regulate my con-
" duct. I thank you, my deareft lady,
" for the fweet· hope you. have given. me.
" I will rely upon it, and. obey your com-
" mands implicitly."—He took her·hand and
kiffed it tenderly.. " Remember, Clement,
" that you are my brother,. and my friend;
" keep within the. limits of thefe rela-
" tions."——

Edith·would not allow. her friend Clement.
to ftay more than one week at the Bower;
fhe told him he. muft then return, and be ready 'to conduct her mother. home; that fhe
wifhed her not to tarry any longer away.

One evening as. they were fitting. after
fupper, Clement mentioned. the adventure
of the wood, and the knight Sir Roland.
Mabel blufhed and fighed at the recollection.
Edith afked him whether he. had gained no
further intelligence of him. " Yes," he
re-

replied; " I have lately been in company
" with Sir Roger Morley, and I inquired af-
" ter Sir Roland; he told me his kinfman
" had mentioned his obligations to me, and
" to the ladies of the name of Calverly.
" ' He longs to fee and to embrace you,'
" faid he, ' and to claim your friendfhip.
" When you fee him next,' faid he, ' you
" muft call him Sir Roger, for that is his
" real name."—

Mabel blufhed a deeper dye---Edith obferved her. " Why," faid fhe, " did he conceal
" his real name?"—" There is a myftery in
" it, I believe; but his kinfman told me I
" fhould one day know him better."——

Mabel fat uneafy while they were fpeaking of Sir Roger, fhe foon after retired to
her own apartment. Edith followed her.
Clement attempted to detain her, but her
prudence prevailed over her wifhes, and fhe
feldom fuffered him to converfe with her
alone. She would not allow him to ftay a
day longer, after the week was elapfed, but
fent him back to the Hall, and defired him
to urge her mother's return.

In

In another week, Clement efcorted Lady Calverly to the Bower, and was allowed to fpend a few more days there.

Edith received her mother with unfeigned joy, Mabel with blufhes and confufion. Lady Calverly embraced her daughters with true maternal affection ; fhe told them that their fifter was perfectly recovered, and fhe left Sir John quite happy.

Clement returned home in a few days, and the ladies refumed their ufual employments and amufements.

In the courfe of two months a remarkable alteration was feen in Mabel. She loft her appetite and her fpirits, fhe grew pale and thin, fhe was filent and referved, and frequently fighed deeply. Edith's eye was upon her, fhe hardly dared tell herfelf the fears and doubts that entered her bofom.

Mabel often retired to her clofet, and ftaid there till fhe was called down ftairs. Edith fometimes followed her thither, but finding the door faftened on the infide, fhe would not intrude herfelf farther. One day fhe went foftly into Mabel's room, fhe was in the clofet, but the door was partly open.

She

She saw her sister shedding tears over a picture which she held in her hand; she wept
even to sobbing, and seemed in great distress.
After observing her some time, and finding
no abatement of her grief, she went into the
closet. She threw her arms round her sister and thus spoke: "My dearest Mabel,
"what can have happened to overwhelm
"you thus with grief? If you deny me the
"knowledge of it, suffer me, at least, to
"weep with you."—

Mabel was struck with this tender expos-
tulation, she returned the sisterly embrace.
"Oh, my sister! my friend! I do not de-
"serve your tenderness. I have been re-
"served to you, and unjust to your friend-
"ship, but I could not help it; I could not
"tell you all my secrets; I dare not."—

"Dare not! surely you could not fear
"me? You could not doubt my affection or
"fidelity?"—"No, no; I did not; but"—
"But what?"—"But I was forbidden."—
"Forbidden! by whom?"—"By one that
"had a right to forbid me."—"Who could
"that be?"—"I cannot tell you. Oh sis-
"ter! sister! the pain in my heart that I
"once

" once talked of, is come upon me in earneſt.
" It oppreſſes me! it kills me!"——She
fainted away. Edith ſupported her, ſhe
ſeated her in a chair, ſhe wept over her.

Mabel revived, ſhe ſaw her ſiſter's concern, ſhe caſt an affecting look towards her
that melted Edith's heart. " Oh, my ſiſter!
" what can I do for you ?"---" Nothing ;
" leave me to my fate."---" Surely, my
" dear, if you would open your heart to
" me, you would find yourſelf relieved, and
" I might think on ſomething to help
" you."---" No, that cannot be."---" Your
" mother, perhaps you will tell her what
" grieves you ?"---" If you love me, if you
" pity me, do not tell my mother, ſhe will
" know too ſoon."---" My ſiſter, you ter-
" rify me! what muſt be known, cannot be
" known too ſoon."---" Oh, no, no! huſh,
" no more! this is too much for me. Dear
" Edith, ſay not a word of this converſa-
" tion: pity me, and love me, and that will
" help me to ſupport myſelf."---" I do both
" moſt truly : try if you cannot make me of
" ſome ſervice to you ; believe that there is
" nothing I would not do or forbear to make
" you eaſy."---

                              " I know.

" I know that you are all goodnefs and
" kindnefs. I thank you, my fifter; I feel
" myfelf better. I will bear up and have
" better hopes."---" Confider whether you
" are right to keep your troubles from a fif-
" ter who loves you, who wifhes to be your
" comforter, and for your own fake put it
" into the power of your friends to ferve
" you."---" I will confider of it. I will
" pray to the Bleffed Virgin to affift and pro-
" tect me. Leave me now, my fifter. I
" will pray and compofe my mind, that I
" may be fit to appear at dinner. I thank
" you for your goodnefs to me."——

Edith left her with a heavy heart, oppreffed with fears for her fifter, and ftill more
for her mother. " If," faid fhe to herfelf;
" if my fifter's honour is loft, it will kill
" my mother, and, perhaps, caufe the death
" of my brother; I muft keep my fears to
" myfelf whatever I may fuffer inwardly."---

Edith affumed a cheerfulnefs that was not
a native of her heart; fhe tried to turn her
mother's attention from Mabel, whofe looks
fhewed a deep melancholy, with an affumed
refolution to conceal from every one the

caufe

cauſe of it. At length Lady Calverly
obſerved the alteration in Mabel's health,
and in her perſon alſo. She mentioned it to
Edith, and was in fear that ſhe was in a decline. Edith could not conceal her concern;
ſhe ſaid, her ſiſter was certainly in ill health,
but ſhe hoped not in a dangerous way.
" She has loſt her appetite, my dear, and
" looks ſtrangely, I think; I will conſult
" Alice, and we will prepare medicines for
" her: I am very much concerned about
" her."---Edith was diſtreſſed, ſhe feared to
ſay too much or too little; ſhe wiſhed that
ſomething might lead to a diſcovery that
might put an end to her anxiety. My Lady
was ſhut up ſome hours with her houſekeeper; in the courſe of their converſation
Alice thought it proper to tell her lady the
hiſtory of Mabel's elopement; and to fix
the date of her complaints, ſhe remarked
upon the ſymptoms of her diſorder, and by
degrees unfolded her ſuſpicions of the cauſe.

Never was aſtoniſhment greater than that
of Lady Calverly; grief, indignation, maternal affection, all were ſtruggling in her
boſom; ſhe could not for ſome time find
words

words to utter her diftrefs. At length fhe
fpoke: " Why was this circumftance fo
" long concealed from me?"---" It was by
" Madam Edith's defire; fhe thought it
" would vex you, and, therefore, defired
" me not to fpeak of it."---

" She might mean it well, but fhe judged
" wrong. I will fpeak to Edith."---Alice
excufed herfelf for her filence. Lady Calverly bade her bring Edith to her directly.
She came at the firft fummons; her mother
accufed her of keeping from her a fecret that
it behoved her much to know.

Edith gave a true and fimple narrative of
all that fhe knew. She fpoke of her fifter's
referves to her from that time; but fhe did
not mention the conference fhe had lately
held with Mabel. She faid that fhe had perceived that her fifter was melancholy and unhappy. She implored her mother to have
pity upon her, to fpeak mildly to her, to invite her to put confidence in her: " If you
" fhould alarm and terrify her," faid fhe,
" you may lofe a child that deferves both
" your love and your pity."—Lady Calverly
burft into a paffion of tears, in which fhe

was

was accompanied by both her auditors.
Edith faw her mother foftened, fhe feized
the moment. " Let me implore you, my
" honoured mother, not to fpeak to Mabel
" till to-morrow; fuffer her to take her reft,
" and take that time for your own reflec-
" tions; let me watch by your bedfide, and
" be your attendant and comforter."—" You
" are that already, my beft Edith; but I can-
" not deprive you of your reft: Oh, how
" can I take any when the honour of my
" family is at ftake ?"—" Then fuffer me to
" fleep with you, my deareft mother, or
" elfe to watch with you; you muft not
" deny me this favour." — " My beloved
" daughter, my friend and counfellor; I
" will repofe my cares in thy gentle bofom,
" it is there only that I can truft them. But
" what muft I do with my unhappy child ?
" I cannot fee her without her perceiving
" my trouble; I cannot fee her as I ufed to
" do."—" Then I will fay you are indif-
" pofed, and you will retire early to your
" own apartment. To-morrow, when you
" have determined on your behaviour, we
" will go to her bedchamber."—" I will fol-
" low

" low your advice, my dearest—alas, how
" shall I bear the thought of my child's
" ruin, and my dishonour ?"—"Take com-
" fort, my dear mother : things may not be
" so bad as you fear : but now let me go to
" my sister; I will attend you when she
" goes to bed."——

Edith met her sister at supper ; she ate nothing, the tears rolled down her face, but
she said nothing to alarm her on her own account, but that her mother was not well,
and that she should sleep with her.

Mabel desired that she might attend her :
but Edith said she must not be disturbed to-
night, but would see her on the morrow. Mabel expressed concern and anxiety. Edith
wished her good repose, and retired.

Lady Calverly and her beloved daughter
watched the whole night; Edith used all
her influence to soften her mother towards
her sister ; she confessed that her suspicions
fell upon their guest Sir Roland, that he had
stolen Mabel's affections, and seduced her
from the path of duty. " Base and unwor-
" thy man, to make such a return for our
" kindness and hospitality ! how dared he to
" seduce

"feduce a daughter of Sir Hugh Calverly,
" and think to go unpunifhed !"---

" Have patience, my deareft mother. As
" far as conjecture goes, it feems to me that
" marriage was his aim, and, perhaps, he
" may have obtained it."---

" God knows whether that be true or not,
" it is only conjecture; but who is this Sir
" Roland? I fear only an adventurer, whom
" nobody knows."—" Have better hopes,
" Madam; Sir Roger Morley has owned
" his relation to our friend, Clement Wood-
" ville, and that he would fhortly claim his
" friendfhip and acknowledge his fervices."—
" There is too much myftery about him;
" a man of plain and decided character needs
" none; I expect the worfe that can befal,
" and arm myfelf againft it."——

In converfation of this kind, the night
paft away; as foon as daylight appeared,
the ladies arofe from a reftlefs pillow. It
was the vernal equinox, the fun rofe at fix
o'clock, and foon after the ladies, attended by
Alice, went to Mabel's apartment.

Edith firft entered the room, with intention to prevent her being furprifed; fhe in-

2   quired

quired after her health, and how she had
rested. Mabel said, " How does my dearest
" mother ? If she is well, no matter for
" me."—" Perhaps," said Edith, " her health
" may depend upon your's; she observes
" that you are not well; she comes to in-
" quire into the cause of your ill health, and
" to consult on the best means of restoring
" you."—" Alas !" said Mabel, " that is
" worse to me than enduring what I have
" brought upon myself."---

Lady Calverly had heard all that passed between her daughters; she came forward, she
looked sternly upon Mabel, whose consci-
ence forestalled the reproof she feared; she
shrunk under the bed-clothes and hid herself. Edith whispered her mother, " Be
" gentle, my dear mother; be tender to
" your Mabel; harshness may bring con-
" sequences that you would hereafter grieve
" to remember; but you never will repent of
" kindness."---

" I know not what to say or do," said my
Lady aloud; " would you have me pass over
" as a light offence, the indiscretion, the
" crime, the dishonour of my child, the
" shame

" shame of my family? I cannot, I will not
" do so."—

Mabel heard what her mother said: she
raised her head and saw her in distress; the
tears rolled down her cheeks, and she leaned
upon Edith as if she was her only support:
she gave a shriek, she jumped out of bed,
and naked as she was, threw herself upon
her knees; she embraced those of her mother; she sobbed deeply, and strove to speak,
but could not immediately. " Oh, my mo-
" ther! oh, my sister! I am not so guilty
" as you suppose me! I have not shamed
" my family! no, indeed I have not! I am
" married --- lawfully married --- I am in-
" deed !"—

" Married !" said Lady Calverly; " mar-
" ried, did you say? How?---when?---where?
" ---to whom?"—" To Sir Roger de Cla-
" rendon; he is my wedded lord and hus-
" band."—" The secret is out," said Edith;
" thank heaven it is no worse! my dear sis-
" ter go into bed again; you will take cold;
" you will be sick: let us talk over these
" matters at leisure; compose yourself, my
" dear Mabel; my mother will hear you,

" she

" she will pity and forgive you."---Lady
Calverly sat down in a chair by the bedside:
the housekeeper and Edith assisted Mabel,
who was near fainting; they put her to bed
again, and Alice went to fetch some water to
give her.   She revived, she seized one of her
mother's hands and bathed it with her tears :
she wept over her, and an affecting pause
succeeded.   Edith feared for them both; she
wished this interview was over; she first
broke silence. " Oh, my mother ! speak to
" your children. Speak a word of comfort to
" your Mabel, and that will comfort your
" Edith, and give vent to your own emo-
" tions."---" What can I say ? Alas ! I am
" convinced of Mabel's situation ! I pray to
" God that she may be married ! who is this
" man who leaves her to sustain alone the
" dreadful trial ? Can he be a man of honour
" or tenderness ?"---

" Yes, indeed, he is both," said Mabel ;
" he is unavoidably absent, on business of
" the greatest consequence to us both ; but
" he will return as soon as possible ; he will
" demand his wife, and excuse his own con-
" duct."---

" I re-

" I remember the name. When your no-
" ble father, Sir Hugh Calverly, was Go-
" vernor of Calais, Sir Roger de Clarendon,
" then a youth, ferved under him in
" the defence of that city; he was highly
" fpoken of as the refemblance of his illuf-
" trious father, the Black Prince, both in
" perfon, courage, and courtefy: but his
" conduct towards Sir Hugh's family does
" not agree with that character; it is that
" of a robber; it is bafe, and unworthy of a
" knight of honour and gallantry."---" My
" dear mother, it is the fame perfon that was
" your gueft, and who affumed the name of
" Sir Roland," faid Edith.---" So much the
" worfe; concealment always implies fome-
" thing wrong: he wronged our friendfhip;
" he ufed our kindnefs and hofpitality to ef-
" fect his own bafe purpofes."---

" Oh !" faid Mabel, " I cannot hear him
" wronged without anfwering for him; let
" me rife, and I will give you proofs of his
" honour and fidelity."---She rofe, and Alice
affifted her in putting on her cloaths. Edith
faid, " You know, Madam, he was wound-
" ed, and in danger of death when he was

" brought

" brought hither ; he certainly did not come
" here with any intention to do us an inju-
" ry ; let us endeavour to think the best
" of him ; if he is our relation, he will make
" himself appear worthy of our alliance ; he
" will acquit himself of these heavy charges :
" let us wait to hear what he can say for
" himself."---" That is kindly said, my dear
" Edith, and I thank you in his behalf."---
" Why did he feign himself dumb ? I see no-
" thing but treachery and deceit in his whole
" conduct." ---" He will one day justify
" himself to you, Madam, and to every
" part of the family ; in the mean time, I
" beseech you to spare him for my sake."---
Mabel went into her closet ; she brought out
a gold ring and a diamond one. " This, Ma-
" dam, is my wedding ring ; and this is a dia-
" mond of great value, which the late Prince
" of Wales gave to my husband's mother, and
" she left it to her son."---

My Lady examined them both. On the
inside of the gold ring there was a posy——

This and the giver are thine for ever. R. C.

" This

" This looks like a proof: but where
" were you married, and by whom?"---
" At Sir Roger's own house, which his fa-
" ther purchased for him many years ago.
" Sir Nicholas Baſſet lately lived in it; but
" in his abſence he deſired his friend to uſe
" it for his ſervice. Sir Roger came thither
" with Maſter Bertram Clifton, and Robert
" Seagrave, his 'ſquires and truſty friends:
" I met him at Hobſon's cottage, and he
" took me from thence."---" And who mar-
" ried you?"---" Father Auſtin, Sir Nicho-
" las Baſſet's chaplain. Maſter Thomas
" Baſſet and the other gentlemen were the
" witneſſes."---

" This is ſome ſatisfaction; but not yet
" ſufficient, till Sir Roger owns his marri-
" age, and accounts for his conduct."---
" Here then let us reſt," ſaid Edith, " till
" this ſatisfaction can be obtained. Both
" of you have ſuffered from this interview;
" it is time to put an end to it. I entreat
" you to compoſe your minds, and wait the
" event with patience."———

Mabel went again to her cloſet; ſhe
brought out her pearl bracelets: ſhe ſhewed

her

her mother the pictures, and she recognized the resemblances.

Mabel threw herself at her feet, and implored her forgiveness: my Lady embraced her, and they sealed the reconciliation with tears. Edith took a part in this renewal of affection: she separated them soon after; she went from one to the other all the day, and sent them early to their repose.

The next day all the parties were much better; the explanation had eased their minds, and their confidence in each other was renewed and confirmed.

Mabel learned that Alice had communicated her suspicions to her mother, and she resented it. Edith convinced her that what was necessary to be known, could not be too soon revealed, and that in regard to her own peace, a mother ought to know all, that she might be able to comfort and support her.

My Lady expressed great displeasure against Hobson and his wife. Mabel excused them at her own expence. Edith proposed a compromise, that Mabel should excuse the housekeeper, and my Lady should forgive the Hobsons: she was the friend, the media-

mediator, the comforter of her mother and fister.

Within a short time after the explanation, Mr. Clement Woodville came to the Bower. Lady Calverly wanted a trufty friend; she meditated, feared, doubted, but at length she refolved to employ him in her fervice.

She told him that she had been very uneafy of late; that she wanted a friend to inquire into certain particulars of the utmoft confequence to her peace.

Clement offered his fervices to the utmoft extent of his power; he would go to ever fo great diftance, through any country whatever; he fhould be mortified if she fhould employ any perfon but himfelf.

After fome prefacing, my Lady told him, that her gueft, whom he had refcued from death, was Sir Roger de Clarendon, the natural fon of the late Prince of Wales. Clement on his part told her all that he had learned from Sir Roger Morley his kinfman, and that he had fince heard that he was gone to court, with a refolution to prefent himfelf to the King, and to claim his protection. My Lady was not difpleafed with this intel-

H 4 ligence.

ligence. She told him that Sir Roger had gained Mabel's affections; that he had, perfuaded her to elope with him, and that she had reafon to think they were privately married : that she was afraid to tell all that she knew to Sir John Calverly, left he should think himfelf obliged to call Sir Roger to account, and to ha▓▓d one or both of their lives : that as Sir Roger was already under obligations to him, he might well be allowed to queftion him on this important fuhject, and to learn of him whether he was married, or whether he intended to marry Mabel : that he muft keep this fecret carefully from Sir John, and let her know what lights he had obtained into this bufinefs : that he fhould fend meffengers from time to time to herfelf only; and that she fhould defray all the expences incurred upon her account, and fhould moreover be under fuch obligation to him, as she should ever acknowledge, and make it her ftudy to promote his intereft and happinefs.

Clement feized the opportunity to ferve Lady Calverly; he affured her of his fecrecy, honour, and fidelity, and of his affiduity in her fervice.

He

He acquainted Edith with all that had paffed between him and her mother; fhe was
pleafed that he was the perfon chofen for
this employment; fhe trufted in his gentlenefs and difcretion to conciliate the friendfhip of Sir Roger de Clarendon, whereas a
warmer and higher fpirit might exafperate
and provoke an enemy, where fhe wifhed to
find a relation and friend.

Clement left the Bower very foon after,
furnifhed with advice and inftructions of
every kind. He went firft to Calverly-hall;
he told Sir John that he was invited to vifit
his brother in London, and offered to exe-
cute any commiffion or command there, fup-
pofing he fhould ftay fome time.

Mabel would not appear below ftairs
while Clement was at the Bower; fhe did
not choofe to fee any man out of the family.
Lady Calverly by degrees treated her with
the fame kindnefs and affection as heretofore.
Edith was the angelic minifter of peace on
all fides.

Within a month from his arrival in London, Clement difpatched a letter to the Bower with the following intelligence:

CLE-

CLEMENT WOODVILLE *to Lady* CALVERLY.

" MOST HONOURED LADY,

" I HAVE loft no time in obeying your
" commands, according to my plan which
" I fhewed your ladyfhip before I left you.
" I am happily enabled to fend you tidings
" of confequence. Sir Roger de Clarendon
" hath prefented himfelf before the King,
" who hath received him gracioufly, ac-
" knowledged him for his brother, and be-
" ftowed many gifts upon him, with pro-
" mifes of farther promotion. Something
" hath happened which forwarded his recep-
" tion wonderfully. The Lord John Hol-
" land hath affaffinated Sir Ralph Stafford ;
" the former is Sir Roger's greateft enemy,
" the latter his fworn friend, and a man in
" great favour with the King : his highnefs
" was in great wrath and fwore he would
" give the murderer up to the law.

" The Princefs Dowager threw herfelf
" upon her knees before the King, and im-
" plored him to fpare the life of her fon.
" He

" He would not grant her requeſt: he ſaid,
" that this was not the priſoner's firſt of-
" fence; that he protected a ſet of deſpera-
" does, who were ready to take away any
" man's life that was obnoxious to him;
" that Sir Ralph Stafford was his good ſer-
" vant, and he would not pardon his mur-
" derer.

" The Princeſs roſe from her knees in
" great anger and reſentment; ſhe ſaid,
" ' Since I cannot prevail with one of my
" ſons, to ſpare the life of another, it is
" time for me to die.'——She went away di-
" rectly, went home, took to her bed, and
" it is thought that ſhe will die with grief.
" Now, my good Lady, you muſt underſtand
" that the Princeſs of Wales hath always
" been the enemy of Sir Roger de Claren-
" don, though he was born long before ſhe
" was married to the Prince. She was jea-
" lous of his father's affection for him, fear-
" ing that he ſhould intercept his favours
" to her ſons, by the Lord Holland, her firſt
" huſband. Her younger ſon, the Lord
" John Holland, took up·an unjuſt aver-
" ſion to Sir Roger, and hath always been

H.6   " his

" his enemy and persecutor. By what I can
" learn, and what I conjecture, it was two
" of his servants that attacked Sir Roger in
" the wood; and now all his bad actions are
" brought to light: he is imprisoned, and it
" is thought the King will suffer the law to
" take its course. These enemies being re-
" moved, Sir Roger hath free access to the
" King, and he is at court every day. I
" have not yet waited upon him, left he
" should think I presume upon the services
" I had the good fortune to render him.
" My brother, Sir Richard, has promised
" to present me to the King, and I am de-
" sirous to see whether Sir Roger will re-
" member me in his presence. As soon as
" I have had a conference with him, I will
" write again, and send a messenger as your
" Ladyship has given me orders.

" My duty and my services attend the fair
" ladies at the Bower.

" I am their's, and your faithful servitor,
" CLEMENT WOODVILLE."

This letter gave great satisfaction to Lady
Calverly; she found it agree with what Mabel

bel had told her; she communicated it to Edith, but she thought proper to keep it from Mabel, till she knew whether Sir Roger would acknowledge his engagement: they both waited with some impatience for another letter from their friend Clement.

Within a fortnight the expected messenger arrived at the Bower, where he was welcomed and entertained as his tidings deserved.

Second Letter from CLEMENT WOODVILLE to Lady CALVERLY.

" MY good Lady, I am impatient to tell
" you what I hope will remove your care
" and anxiety. Sir Roger de Clarendon is a
" man of honour and principle; he owns his
" marriage, and glories in it: I tell you
" this most happy circumstance before I de-
" scend to particulars.

" My brother carried me to court as he
" promised; Sir Roger was there. Sir Ri-
" chard said to the King—' I beg your High-
" ness's permission to present my brother,
" Clement Woodville, to you; he will be

I   " proud

" proud to receive your Highnefs's com-
" mands.'—Sir Roger ftepped forward, I had
" the honour to kifs the King's hand ; when
" I rofe up, Sir Roger came up to me, he
" took my hand—' Mr. Clement Wood-
" ville I rejoice to meet you here. My Lord
" the King, I am more obliged to this gen-
" tleman than to any man living ; he faved
" my life when I was left in the wood, co-
" vered with wounds, and almoft expiring;
" but befide this, he is one of the braveft,
" the tendereft, and the worthieft of men.'—
" The King honoured me fo far as to thank
" me for my fervices to his brother ; he
" bade my brother remind him of me, and
" think of fomething for him to do for me.
" I was overcome by his gracioufnefs. I
" thanked his Highnefs ; I faid I wifhed to
" be in a fituation to fhow my gratitude and
" obedience.——Sir Roger took me afide,
" he afked me where I lodged ; I told him
" at my brother's, and hoped to fee him
" there, for I had fome things to communi-
" cate that required privacy : he promifed to
" come the next day, and we parted.

" My brother and I retired ; I told him of
" our adventure in the wood, of Sir Roger's
" fick-

" ficknefs and recovery, and of his obliga-
" tions to Lady Calverly and her fair daugh-
" ters; but not the leaft hint of my com-
" miffion.

" The next day Sir Roger came to my
" brother's houfe; we had a long conference
" together, of which I referve the particu-
" lars for your private ear; but I can with
" confidence affure you, that he is all that
" ever you have heard of him. He honours.
" your Ladyfhip; he doats upon your daugh-
" ter Mabel; he is impatient to throw him-
" felf at your feet, and to claim his
" efpoufed bride. He has promifed to de-
" clare his marriage to the King the firft op-
" portunity, and after that he will write to
" his lady; his letter will be fent by the.
" next meffenger, and one of mine will.
" come at the fame time.

" With my duty and my prayers for your
" Ladyfhip and family, I remain,

" Your moft faithful and humble fervitor,

" C. WOODVILLE."

Lady

Lady Calverly was overjoyed at the tidings in this letter. Edith begged her to communicate the contents of both letters to Mabel, faying, " She has fuffered enough, " and now fhe ought to know her own hap- " pinefs."—

My Lady could not refufe this requeft, and Edith prepared her fifter by degrees to hear what fo nearly concerned her. She bore it with great compofure, faying, fhe never doubted her hufband's honour or fidelity.

My Lady was profufe in the praife of Clement : his coolnefs, his judgement, his difcretion, were the fubject of her eulogy. Edith enjoyed his praifes ; Mabel fometimes caft an arch look at her ; but fhe joined in commending him without the leaft difcompofure, and applauded her mother's choice of a friend and confident.

A fhort time after, Clement's third meffenger arrived ; he brought two letters, which were highly fatisfactory to all the ladies at the Bower.

Third

Third Letter of CLEMENT WOODVILLE *to*
Lady CALVERLY.

" HONOURED AND BELOVED LADY,
" I SALUTE you refpectfully, and pre-
" fume to congratulate you and myfelf on,
" the good fuccefs of my embaffy.

" I have now to inform you that the
" Princefs of Wales is dead, and the court
" have put on the appearance of mourning
" and grief. Some do blame the King for
" refufing to grant his mother the life of her
" fon ; others admire his refolution to refufe
" to pardon the murderer of his fervant, for
" that would have been to encourage fuch
" atrocious actions ; and he ought to protect
" the lives of his people, and fuffer the law
" to take its courfe.

" The Lord Thomas Holland fent a mef-
" fage to know whether he might wait on
" the King; he was told he might, and
" fhould be welcome. He came in deep
" mourning, with his eyes full of tears ;
" he kneeled to the King, who raifed and
" embraced him, and called him his dear bro-
" ther.

" ther. They wept together for the death
" of their mother, and the King shewed
" great concern.

" The Lord Holland took the time when
" the King was softened; he said his un-
" happy brother John was become a forfeit
" of the law, that he implored his Highnefs
" to grant him a reprieve for fome time,
" that he might have time to repent of his
" crimes, and prepare for death. He urged his
" fuit with fo much grief and humility,
" that the King could not refufe it. He
" gave him a reprieve for three months, in
" the courfe of which the Lord Holland
" hopes to obtain his pardon. Whether he
" will fucceed is yet uncertain; in the mean
" time the imprifonment of the Lord John
" is of great advantage to Sir Roger de Cla-
" rendon, for it was he who hindered his ac-
" cefs to the King; he did him many ill
" offices in other refpects: he encouraged
" a dependent of his, by name John Soun-
" der, to pretend that he was a fon of the
" late Prince of Wales, and to fet forth his
" pretenfions as equal to thofe of Sir Roger.
" He employed his emiffaries to flander and
" ca-

" calumniate his character ; and, finally, he
" told the King that Sir Roger was gone to
" Paleſtine on a pilgrimage to the Holy Se-
" pulchre, intending by his inſtrument to
" have him aſſaſſinated in England. This
" was the cauſe of Sir Roger's concealment,
" and of his pretending to be dumb, in order
" to evade all inquiries. He will give you
" himſelf all the particulars of his life, when
" he is ſo happy to wait on your Ladyſhip.
" For this time I humbly take my leave, and
" remain,

" Your true and faithful ſervant,

" C. WOODVILLE."

Letter from Sir ROGER DE CLARENDON *to*
Lady CALVERLY.

" MOST NOBLE, GENEROUS, AND
" HONOURABLE LADY,

" I LEARN from Mr. Clement Wood-
" ville, my dear and worthy friend, that you
" have been under much care and anxiety,
" of which I am in ſome meaſure the cauſe.
" That your fair daughter Mabel hath been

2   " ſick

" fick in body and mind, and being urged
" by you, fhe hath confeffed her engage-
" ment to you. I declare to you, my good
" Lady, that I claim the honour to be her
" hufband, and that I will demand her of
" you, as foon as I have prepared an houfe
" fit to receive her. My enemies have long
" kept me from having accefs to the King,
" upon whom I depend, in a great degree,
" for my rank and fortune.

" It pleafed God that I fhould at length
" find a time when my enemies were put
" afide, and the King hath acknowledged
" me for his brother, and promifed to pro-
" vide for me. The Princefs of Wales is
" dead, the Lord Holland is in prifon ; he is
" convicted of a bafe and treacherous mur-
" der, and his life depends on the breath of
" the King. God forbid that I fhould tri-
" umph in their misfortunes! I lament and
" pity them ; but I truft it is out of their
" power to do me any farther injury.

" I cannot at prefent leave the King ; but
" as foon as I can do it properly, I will wait
" upon you and my dear Lady. I hope you
" will own me for a fon, and Madam Edith
" for

" for a brother, feeing that the fweet Mabel
" acknowledges me for her hufband, which is
" my pride and glory.

" When I leave the court, I will wait on
" Sir John Calverly, in my way to the Bow-
" er, till which time I could wifh he might
" not know of my marriage; but I refer
" this point to your Ladyfhip's difcretion.

" Salute my deareft Mabel for me, and
" bid her depend on my conftant affection
" and fidelity: I remember your family
" always in my prayers, and beg your's for
" me, and I remain,

" Your fon and fervant,

" ROGER DE CLARENDON."

This letter made Lady Calverly's mind
eafy; till this time fhe had not been without fears of Sir Roger's integrity: but fhe
was now freed from all doubts and cares for
her daughter. Mabel triumphed in her hufband's fidelity, and in her reliance upon his
honour. My Lady had forborne to reproach
her with her indifcretion, at Edith's requeft;
but

but now she told her all the danger she had incurred, and the troubles she might have brought upon her family. Mabel asked pardon, but yet she would not give up the idea, that it was her fate to act as she did, and she could in no wise have helped it.

Fourth Letter of CLEMENT WOODVILLE *to Lady* CALVERLY.

" HONOURED AND DEAR LADY,

" SIR Roger writes to assure you of his
" honour, and of his attention to your
" daughter's interest and happiness. He de-
" sires me to give you an account of some
" things that have passed that are of confe-
" quence to him; for he is paying his court
" to the King daily, and is using the oppor-
" tunity of the absence of his enemies to
" establish his own fortunes.

" When a man is in trouble and difgrace,
" his enemies declare his faults, and his
" friends betray him. So is it with the
" Lord John Holland; one of his emiffaries
" hath confeffed that himfelf and John Soun-

" der

" der afore-mentioned, were the men that
" attacked Sir Roger in the wood near your
" Bower, and that they did it by the order of
" the Lord John Holland; moreover he
" faid, he knew where the faid John Soun-
" der and his affociates were concealed.

" Sir Roger defired that they might be
" taken prifoners and brought to town to be
" examined farther. The King approved it,
" and the Lord Mayor gave his warrant to
" apprehend them. I offered to go with the
" party to take them, and Mafter Bertram
" Clifton refolved to do the fame : accord-
" ingly we went, and found them where we
" were directed. They made fome refiftance,
" but were overpowered and brought to
" London; the King defired to hear their
" examination, fo they were brought to
" court the next day.

" The King defired to fee John Sounder,
" fo he ftood forth. ' I afk you by what
" authority you dare to call yourfelf the fon
" of my father ?' faid the King.—' By the
" authority of my mother,' anfwered the
" man, ' who I fuppofe was likely to
" know.'—' Who was your mother, was fhe
" mar-

" married or fingle ?'—' She was the wife of
" an archer called John Sounder, as I am,
" and he was in the fervice of my Lord the
" Prince of Wales.'—' Did the Prince own
" you ? Did he declare to any man of credit
" that you were his fon ?'—' I cannot tell
" whether he did or not.'—' Did he ever tell
" you fo ?'—The man was filent. ' Speak,
" fellow; anfwer me.'—' I cannot fay he
" did ; but I have as good a right to believe
" that I am his fon, as Sir Roger de Claren-
" don.'—' No, you have not. My father
" acknowledged him to all the world, even
" to my mother, before he married her: he
" prefented him to the King my grandfather,
" who knighted him; and he would have
" owned you alfo, if you had really been his
" fon.'—

" The Lord John Beauchamp was prefent,
" he came forward and fpoke:

" ' I beg your Highnefs's permiffion to
" fay a few words in behalf of my royal maf-
" ter, in whofe fervice I fpent the beft part
" of my life. He was a good as well as a
" great man. He would have fcorned to fe-
" duce the wife of any man ; he would
" fooner

" fooner have died than have been guilty of
" fuch an action.

"I beg leave to fpeak a word of Sir Ro-
" ger de Clarendon, who is the true fon of
" my noble mafter. His mother was a young
" lady of birth and merit, whom he ref-
" cued from great diftrefs after the taking of
" Calais. He never had any other concu-
" bine befide her; fhe bore him a fon and a
" daughter, who is now the wife of Valeran
" de Luxemburg, Count of St. Pol. He
" acknowledged both thefe children to all
" his friends, and even to the world. By
" his laft will and teftament he bequeathed
" to Sir Roger de Clarendon his natural
" fon, a fine filk bed, and all the furniture
" of one room, a part of his wardrobe, and
" a legacy in money befide. Thefe are folid
" proofs, and cannot be fet afide. This fel-
" low is an impoftor, who, out of envy and
" malice to Sir Roger de Clarendon, hath
" pretended to be the fon of the late Prince:
" but I hope, my Liege, you will punifh
" him for this, and for the other crimes he
" hath been guilty of; the flander of your
" noble father is what I cannot ftand by and

" hear filently, and were he a man of credit
" and character, I would make him eat his
" words, but as an aſſaſſin and a villain, I
" leave him to your Highneſs, and to the
" law.'—

" The King took my Lord Beauchamp by
" the hand, he thanked him for defending
" his father's character, and aſſented to all
" that he had faid.

" He ordered that John Sounder ſhould be
" impriſoned, and that he ſhould be tried
" for his offences by the law; if that ſpared
" his life, he ſhould be baniſhed for ever
" from this realm of England. He forbade.
" him to call himſelf the ſon of the Prince
" of Wales from henceforth for ever; and
" he bade the Mayor's officers take him out
" of his preſence. While they were taking
" him away, the man faid, they could not
" hinder him to think himſelf the Prince's
" ſon, and that he ſhould do while he lived.

" I was preſent at this ſcene, and I thought
" your Ladyſhip would like to hear it, be-
" cauſe it proves Sir Roger's pretenſions to
" the honour of being the ſon of the moſt
" noble Prince of Wales, and the King's re-
" gard for him.

" He

" He defires me to ftay fome time longer
" in London, until he can conveniently re-
" turn with me, which he is impatient to
" do.

" We fhall go firft to Calverly-hall to
" wait on Sir John, and from thence to the
" Bower of peace and contentment. I wifh
" ardently for the time, and remain,

" Your Ladyfhip's moft dutiful,

" And humble fervant,

" C. WOODVILLE."

Lady Calverly detained the meffenger till
fhe fhould write anfwers to both the letters,
which fhe got in readinefs on the following
day.

Lady CALVERLY *to Sir* ROGER DE CLA-
RENDON.

" SIR ROGER DE CLARENDON,

" I HAVE received your letter, the con-
" tents whereof have in a great meafure re-

I 2   " moved

" moved my doubts, and given me fatisfac-
" tion.

" You muft allow that I have juft caufe
" of refentment towards you.

" Firft, for feducing the affections of a
" young maiden of an honourable family.—
" Secondly, for marrying her in a clandef-
" tine manner, without the knowledge or
" confent of her mother, or any part of her
" family.—And, thirdly, for leaving her to
" go through a moft fevere trial by herfelf,
" which fhe has fuftained with more courage
" and fortitude than is common to a young
" woman of her years and modefty. I for-
" bear to aggravate thefe charges againft you
" by mentioning the particular circumftances
" of your conduct, while you were fhelter-
" ed under my roof.

" I forgive all that is paft, upon condi-
" tion that you make due amends for it by
" your behaviour as a hufband to my daugh-
" ter Mabel; truly, Sir, fhe deferves that
" you fhould do fo, for fhe has fhewn the
" moft fincere and ardent affection for you,
" and the moft fteady reliance upon your
" honour and fidelity. She wifhes to write
" to

" to you herfelf, but has not yet been taught
" to ufe a pen, which I thought needlefs for
" fo young a woman as herfelf; but fhe
" fhall learn it when her health fhall permit
" and opportunity ferves.

" Now, Sir, I muft fpeak upon a fubject
" which none but your wife's mother could
" mention to you. By my daughter's ac-
" count you have been married full fix
" months: it is ftrange that you fhould not
" have expected that within that time your
" marriage would difcover itfelf. Think
" what your poor Mabel muft have fuffered
" by fuch a difcovery, and what her mother
" muft feel on the occafion; how much the
" hufband's prefence was wanted and wifhed
" to fupport and comfort his efpoufed, but
" not acknowledged wife. Mabel ftood it
" nobly and fteadily, and well deferves to be
" rewarded, as I truft you will own and
" agree to.

" I underftand that you are cultivating
" your intereft with the King, which may
" be right and prudent, but as foon as you
" can leave the court, let us fee you here,
" for your honour can be no where fo much
" concerned.

I 3   " I com-

" I comply with your requeſt in keeping
" ſecrecy towards Sir John againſt my own
" opinion, for I think he cannot know it
", too ſoon. Edith ſalutes you. Mabel
" ſends her love and duty. We all remem-
" ber you in our prayers.

 " I am,

" The friend of your honour and proſperity,

   * ISABEL CALVERLY."

Lady CALVERLY *to* CLEMENT WOOD-
VILLE, *Eſquire.*

" MASTER CLEMENT WOODVILLE,

 " I THANK you heartily for your good
" offices, which have been performed much
" to the credit of your honour and ability;
" they have raiſed you high in my eſteem,
" and I ſhall always be ready to own my
" obligations to you, and to reward your
" ſervices, as opportunity ſhall be given me.
" I am glad to hear that you have been pre-
" ſented to the King, and that his Highneſs
" has deſired to be reminded of you: I wiſh
" and pray that he may provide for you ſoon,

      " for

" for it grows time for you to look forward
" to an eftablifhment for yourfelf. 1 fhall
" confult with Sir John on fome means to
" do you fervice, and I fhall confider you
" as my friend upon this and every other
" occafion.

" Continue, I pray you, to give me an
" account of every thing that bears relation
" to Sir Roger de Clarendon ; I hope he
" will foon be at leifure to come to the
" Bower, and that you will attend him hi-
" ther.

" My daughters falute you, and we re-
" member you in our prayers—farewel,

"""" Your friend to ferve you,

"""""" " ISABEL CALVERLY."

Thefe communications afforded fubjects
of converfation to the ladies at the Bower ;
they gave a new flow of fpirits, increafed
their confidence in each other, and gave fatisfaction to all of them. They united in
wifhes, prayers, and expectations of the arrival of Sir Roger de Clarendon.

The week following another courier arrived with a pacquet of letters.

Sir.

Sir ROGER DE CLARENDON *to Lady* CAL-VERLY.

" HONOURED AND DEAR LADY,

" I THANK you a thoufand times for
" the honour you have done me in fending
" me a letter of your own hand-writing. I
" thank you for all and every part of it,
" even for your corrections, which are thofe
" of a parent and a friend. I fhall endea-
" vour to deferve your good opinion, and
" to anfwer the hopes you have entertained
" of me. After the hint you have given, I
" can no longer delay waiting upon you. I
" have this day informed the King of my
" marriage, and the date of it. He faid this
" alliance was an honour to me ; I anfwered
" that I efteemed it fo. He permitted me
" to wait on the Queen, and I declared the
" fame to her Highnefs, and told her of the
" beauty and merit of the lady I had the ho-
" nour to call by my name. I afked per-
" miffion of the King to vifit my wife and
" her family : he gave it me freely. I fhall
" fet

" set out two days hence: Mr. Clement
" Woodville will accompany me. I have
" ordered my meſſenger to meet me at Cal-
" verly-hall. I ſhall ſtay no longer there,
" than till I have made myſelf known to
" Sir John, and ſaluted him as my brother;
" then I ſhall come to the Bower with all
" ſpeed. I ſhall leave at the court, Maſter
" Bertram Clifton, and Maſter Robert Sea-
" grave, my truſty friends, and they will
" write me word of what paſſes there during
" my abſence, that it concerns me to know.
" Maſter Thomas Baſſet, who was preſent at
" my marriage, will either go with us, or fol-
" low us to Calverly-hall. When I have the
" happineſs to throw myſelf at your ladyſhip's
" feet, I will tell you every circumſtance of
" my life paſt, and whereſoever you ſhall
" think me worthy of blame, I will condemn
" myſelf, and aſk your pardon: you have
" aſſured me of grace and favour, ſo I ſhall
" throw myſelf upon your mercy. In the
" interim, I remain,

" Your Ladyſhip's in all reſpect and duty,

" ROGER DE CLARENDON."

" My

" My beſt love and ſervioe to the fair
" Edith; and to my wife my heart's entire
" affections."

Sir ROGER *to Lady* CLARENDON.

" DEAREST AND MOST BELOVED OF
" WOMEN,

" HAST thou ſuffered by my abſence ?
" Knoweſt thou what I alſo have ſuffered ?
" No, thou doſt not: thy revered mother
" chides me in thy behalf, as if I had ſought
" for an excuſe to be abſent.

" I told thee, my deareſt, that I muſt
" leave thee for a time, in order to obtain
" the means to receive thee according to thy
" birth and merit; this end is now obtained,
" the King owns and protects me, the Queen
" patronizes me.

" When I am ſo happy as to hold thee in
" mine arms, thou ſhalt ſhrive me of all
" my faults, and whereſoever thou findeſt
" me to blame, thou ſhalt enjoin a penance
" ſuitable to the offence; any penance but
" that of an enforced abſence. I leave the

I   " court

" court the day after to-morrow, and hope
" foon to enjoy thy prefence. Now does
" time move with leaden wings, I reckon
" every minute for an hour, and every hour
" as a day, till I fhall behold again my be-
" loved Mabel, my lady, my wife, and my
" heart's treafure. Heaven grant us a happy
" meeting, prays thy faithful lover, and ac-
" knowledged hufband,

" ROGER DE CLARENDON."

Thefe letters excited the impatience of all
the ladies at the Bower; that of Mabel was
a mixture of pleafure and pain, that proved
the infufficiency of earthly happinefs to fa-
tisfy the immortal foul.

The following day the meffenger returned
to meet his mafter at Calverly-hall: within
three days after he came again to the Bower
with another letter.

Fifth Letter of CLEMENT WOODVILLE *to*
Lady CALVERLY.

" I WRITE now to inform your Lady-
" fhip of all that is paffing at the Hall, and

I 6

" to

" to prepare you to receive your long-ex-
" pected and defired gueft.

" Sir Roger de Clarendon, Mr. Thomas
" Baffet, and myfelf, arrived here on Tuef-
" day laft. Sir John received us with his
" accuftomed courtefy and kindnefs. Sir
" Roger faid, he had long wifhed to pay his
" refpect to him, that he had favours to ac-
" knowledge, and favours to afk befide. He
" fpoke of the kindnefs and hofpitality with
" which he was entertained at the Bower,
" and ufed many expreffions of gratitude
" and affection. He mentioned his obliga-
" tions to me, faid that he was bound to me
" by all the ties of friendfhip, and that he
" hoped for my influence with Sir John to
" obtain his alfo, which he fhould efteem
" as an honour, and cultivate with all his
" powers.

" Sir John replied, that he embraced the
" occafion that brought him acquainted with
" fo noble a gentleman, that he accepted his
" friendfhip, and offered his own in return,
" and that he was obliged to the ladies at the
" Bower for the attentions they had paid to
" their noble gueft.—

" Many

" Many more words of ceremony paſſed
" on both ſides, but we did not enter upon
" the important ſubject till the next day.
" After breakfaſt Sir Roger began as follows :
" —' Sir John Calverly, I thank you for
" your generous and kind reception. I told
" you yeſterday that I had favours to ac-
" knowledge, and favours to aſk beſide; I
" ſhall now explain the latter. During my
" reſidence at the Bower, I ſaw daily your
" charming ſiſters; but though I admired
" them both, one only captivated my heart,
" and that was the charming Mabel. I
" ſhould have waited on you immediately to
" have aſked her in marriage, but I was in
" a peculiar ſituation : my enemies were
" lying in wait for my life, and my friends
" were inceſſantly urging me to go to the
" King, and ſhelter myſelf under his pro-
" tection. At further leiſure I will explain
" all the circumſtances, but I will now keep
" to the ſubject of my preſent viſit, which
" is to aſk your conſent to my marriage with
" your ſiſter Mabel.'—Sir John looked ſur-
" priſed. ' Conſent to your marriage, Sir !
" What are you then aſſured of my ſiſter's
" fa-

" favour, of my mother's confent?'—Sir
" Roger bowed gracefully; ' Sir, I have
" the honour and happinefs to be fecure of
" both.'—' Indeed, Sir! it is ftrange that
" my mother fhould not have written to me
" upon the fubject.'—' Why, Sir, fhe has
" alfo been under peculiar circumftances,
" which fhall in due time be explained; but
" let us keep to the prefent occafion. I afk
" your confent, and I will convince you of
" that of the ladies.'—' Sir, if you have ob-
" tained their confent, I have no right to
" withhold mine.' — ' Nor inclination, I
" hope, Sir John?'—' None, I affure you.'—
" ' Then fuffer me to embrace you as my
" brother.'—' Are you then married?'—
" ' Yes, God be thanked!'—Sir John looked
" ferious: ' Surely I ought to have been
" made acquainted, the circumftances re-
" quire explanation.'—' All fhall be explain-
" ed: hear me, Sir John; you have been a
" lover, and ought to excufe a lover's pre-
" cipitate conduct, fuch I confefs was mine.
" I exchanged vows with your lovely fifter
" before I left the Bower; (Sir John frown-
" ed) I went from thence to Sir Nicholas
" Baf-

" Baffet's ; he has rented a houfe of mine for
" three years paft. I there related my ad-
" venture in the wood, the affiftance I re-
" ceived from Mr. Woodville, the hofpita-
" lity of Lady Calverly, the beauty and
" merit of her daughters. Several young
" gentlemen were prefent, they had heard
" of the young ladies, and of their merits :
" two of them avowed intentions to vifit
" them, and to pay court to them. Mr.
" Ralph Baffet, the elder brother of this
" young gentleman here prefent, was one ;
" Mr. Henry Beauchamp the other. My
" heart was enflamed with love and jealoufy.
" I feared that while I was abfent, another
" man might obtain my prize. I wrote to
" Mabel feveral times ; I befought her to
" give me a meeting, which at length fhe
" granted. I urged her to put herfelf under
" my protection : (Here Sir John fhook his
" head) I carried her to Sir Nicholas Baffet's,
" he was abfent, but he had given me leave
" to ufe the houfe as my own. (Sir John bit
" his lip and turned pale) Here I married the
" charming Mabel, the treafure of my life.
" Here I received the moft precious proof
" of

" of her affection and confidence in me,
" which I shall ever consider as the first
" blessing of my life.'—

" ' Who were present? Who married
" you?' said Sir John, with impatience.—
" Sir, I have here an authentic certificate,
" signed by proper witnesses; we were mar-
" ried by Sir Nicholas Basset's chaplain,
" and this young gentleman, Mr. Thomas
" Basset, was one of the witnesses, as he will
" testify.'—Mr. T. Basset then testified his
" presence at the ceremony. Sir John read
" the paper, he returned it to Sir Roger,
" and his countenance was more composed.
" He desired Sir Roger to proceed.——He
" then told him the necessity of his journey
" to London, his wish to conceal his mar-
" riage for a time, and his reasons for it:
" his audience of the King, the machina-
" tions of his enemies, and all that followed
" during his residence in London: his meet-
" ing me there, his writing to Lady Calver-
" ly, her answer, and his impatience to go
" to the Bower: his resolution to visit Sir
" John, and his motives for it: his jour-
" ney here, and his impatience to be at the
                                    " Bower.

" Bower. That he had prevailed upon Mr.
" T. Baffet and me to give him our com-
" pany, that the former might bear witnefs
" to his being honourably and properly mar-
" ried, and that the latter might mediate on
" his behalf in cafe it fhould be neceffary;
" that Lady Calverly knew all, and had for-
" given him, and he hoped Sir John would
" upon the fame condition, namely, that
" his future behaviour to his fifter fhould be
" unexceptionable.——

 " Sir John changed colour feveral times
" in the courfe of his fpeech. When it
" was concluded, he was filent a minute or
" two. I then fpoke with great caution,
" as I thought beft not to mention my com-
" miffion from your Ladyfhip, left Sir John
" fhould fufpeét, that Sir Roger had need to
" be reminded of his duty, and left Sir Ro-
" ger fhould fufpeét, that your Ladyfhip
" was of his opinion. I faid, that after my
" meeting Sir Roger at court, and the re-
" newal of our friendfhip, I had been per-
" mitted to write to Lady Calverly in Sir
" Roger's behalf, and to mediate between
" them: that I was well affured that my
       " Lady

" Lady had forgiven both him and her
" daughter, and that his prefence was impa-
" tiently expected by all the ladies at the
" Bower: that in regard to them, I hoped
" Sir John would not detain him longer
" than was neceffary for his fatisfaction.—

" Sir John recollected himfelf; he rofe
" and embraced Sir Roger, and affured him
" of his friendfhip and brotherly affection:
" he mentioned his fifter's fortune, and of-
" fered to add to it. Sir Roger would not
" hear of it.—They talked upon other fub-
" jects, and were every minute more pleafed
" with each other; and I have the honour
" and pleafure to affure you, they are united
" in the ftrongeft bands of friendfhip.

" All thefe things are better to be known
" before you meet them. We fhall fet out
" out to-morrow, and come with all conve-
" nient fpeed to the Bower, and you will be
" fully prepared to receive us. I claim a
" fhare in the family joy, as one of the moft
" humble, and faithful of its fervants.

" CLEMENT WOODVILLE."

Lady

Lady Calverly was well pleafed with this letter, fhe communicated it to Edith : my Lady was eloquent in Clement's praifes, and Edith did not contradict her. Mabel was agitated by hopes and fears ; fhe wifhed and yet dreaded to fee the lord of her heart. She had been told of men that were capable of neglecting and defpifing their wives, becaufe they were too eafily won. Sir Roger might be one of thefe ; her brother might be difpleafed with her, or her hufband : an hundred caufes of fear opprefs the heart that truly loves, and every thing that relates to the object, gives exquifite pleafure, or the moft poignant anguifh. Edith was the moft tender of friends, and the moft fuccefsful comforter.

The next morning, as the ladies were fitting in the parlour at breakfaft, a knocking was heard at the outward gate. Mabel changed colour. Edith faid, " Be com- " pofed, my fifter ; it is either a fervant, or " a familiar friend, otherwife his coming " would have been announced by the horn." —The door was opened, and Clement Woodville entered the room. They were rejoiced

to

to fee him. He came forward to my Lady,
he took her hand and kiffed it. She faid,
" My friend, you are truly welcome !"—" I
" thank you, Madam; I congratulate you
" on this happy occafion : my dear ladies,
" accept me as an harbinger to ftill more
" welcome guefts. I thought Lady Claren-
" don might be furprifed, therefore I came
" forward at full fpeed to prepare her to fee
" Sir Roger without being difcompofed."—
" You are the moft prudent and confiderate
" of men," faid my Lady : " I am fure all
" of us are under great obligations to you."
—The young ladies joined in the acknow-
ledgement. Clement was all life and fpirits,
he kept them in talk till the found of the
horn was heard at a diftance firft, the fecond
blaft was nearer, the third was in the court-
yard. Mabel was overcome with her emotions, her mother fupported and encouraged
her. Sir John Calverly was the firft man
that came forward, he took Sir Roger's
hand, led him to my Lady. She bowed
her head and pointed to Mabel. Sir Roger
kneeled to her, he kiffed her hand, and that
of her daughter who leaned upon her.

He

He then rofe. " Permit me, Madam, " to fupport the moft welcome burthen that " ever man received into his arms."—He took her from her mother, he embraced her tenderly : he fpoke words of the moft gentle and affectionate nature : he told her he hoped all her fufferings and his own were ended, and they might enjoy, undifturbed, the bleffings which heaven had prepared for them. By degrees fhe recovered, fhe wept in his bofom, and peace returned to her own.

While thefe lovers were thus engaged, the reft of the company faluted and congratulated each other. My Lady thanked Sir John for giving her thus unexpectedly the pleafure of his company. He faid, " I had " not intended it, but Sir Roger urged me " to accompany him in fo earneft a manner, " that I could not refufe him. Your fon- " in-law, Madam, is mafter of the art of " perfuafion ; I do not wonder that Mabel " could not refift him, for I find myfelf un- " able to refute his arguments, or to grant " any requeft he makes me. From this " time forward we are all one family."—

Con-

Congratulations were given and returned on all fides, and never was there feen an happier family than that Eglantine Bower contained. They fpent feveral days together, without a wifh beyond what bleffings were included in that houfe.

Sir John began to look towards thofe he had left at Calverly-hall: Sir Roger would not hear him fpeak of his return at prefent; he requefted him to make a vifit with him to Sir Nicholas Baffet's, he wifhed to introduce that family to his acquaintance and friendfhip, and to defire Sir Nicholas to quit that houfe as foon as he could conveniently. My Lady begged him not to be in hafte, nor yet to hurry his friend; fhe faid that Mabel might remain at the Bower, till it was quite convenient to him to receive her; and that himfelf fhould be the moft welcome gueft and inmate at all times. Sir Roger paid his acknowledgements, and faid he fhould joyfully accept her offer for fome months to come, but he hoped in the fpring to carry his dear wife to her own houfe.

They went to Sir Nicholas Baffet's, they fpent one day and night there; when they return-

returned, they were accompanied by the two young gentlemen, Mr. Ralph, and Mr. Thomas Baffet. Clement's countenance fell at the fight of them, he doubted not the intention of their vifits: he folicited an interview with his adored Edith, and told her his fears and his vexations. Edith affured him of her readinefs in refufing any offer of marriage; fhe owned his merit, and her own attachment to him: fhe faid, things were working about to the point fhe defired; that they muft by patience and fortitude conquer the difficulties in their way, and entitle themfelves to the bleffings that awaited them. She concluded by faying, " Cul- " tivate my mother's friendfhip, and rely " upon my honour and conftancy."—Clement was re-affured; but ftill he had mifgivings in his heart.

This honourable and happy company held many interefting converfations upon various fubjects, which Mr. Clement Woodville committed to writing; for he was fond of reading and writing, more than was common in thofe times.

He.

He thought some things that had been said, might be useful, both to the public, and to private persons, and he wished to revive the remembrance of them for his own benefit and satisfaction.

One day as they were sitting after dinner, Sir John Calverly jested with his sister Edith on her suffering her younger sister to be married before her. She smiling said, she did not feel the least degree of mortification upon that account.

" You know, Edith, it is your own fault;
" you are so hard to be pleased, that it will
" be difficult to find a man that will meet
" with your approbation."—" I believe you
" are right, brother; perhaps I may require
" qualities that are not very common."—

Mr. Ralph Basset asked her to name her requisites, that men might know whether they could answer to them or not.—Edith said, the man she should favour must be a very odd person, " And no man would think
" it worth his while to pretend to such qua-
" lities as I should wish for in a husband."—
" Pray tell us some of them, Edith," said Sir John.—" In the first place he must have
" nei-

" neither pride, vanity, nor ambition."—
" You muſt explain yourſelf farther."—

" Secondly, he muſt love my mother as
" well, or better than myſelf. The truth
" is, I have reſolved never to leave my dear
" mother, conſequently, the man who
" wiſhes to be my huſband, muſt relinquiſh
" all his deſire of promotion, in whatever
" ſituation he may be. He muſt devote him-
" ſelf wholly to the domeſtic duties, he
" muſt be our protector, friend, counſellor,
" and affiſtant, the overlooker of our farm,
" the maſter of our ſervants, and the friend of
" mankind: he muſt, beſide theſe requiſites,
" be able to pleaſe in all other reſpects, and
" to pleaſe one of us ſignifies nothing, for
" we are inſeparable."—

" And where do you expect to find ſuch
" a man, Edith?"—" Why that is my
" ſhield of defence againſt all my offers of
" marriage; I do not expect to meet with
" ſuch a man, nor, perhaps, I do not wiſh
" it; but yet, unleſs I do meet with ſuch a
" one, I will never marry."—" But ſuppoſe
" ſuch a man as you could like in other
" reſpects were to offer, but that having al-

" ready taken a profeſſion upon him, he
" could not defert his ſtation without a
" blemiſh upon his charaſter. A foldier,
" for inſtance."—" Oh, I would not marry
" a foldier upon any earthly confideration.
" What agonies of hopes and fears ſhould I
" have to undergo, while he was abſent upon
" duty! and when he returned, with his
" brows crowned with a wreath of falſe
" glory, I ſhould fancy I faw him bathed
" in the blood of his fellow-creatures; and
" I ſhould ſhrink from his ſight and touch."
—" Oh fie, Edith! recolleſt that you are
" the daughter of a foldier, a man equally
" brave and humane; a man refpeſted and
" beloved."—" I revere the memory of my
" father; but you were ſpeaking of a huſ-
" band: while I am unmarried I may choofe,
" and I may refufe; I declare againſt a fol-
" dier."—

" I perceive that you mean to live fingle,
" and that you would objeſt to every man
" and every profeſſion." — " Perhaps not,
" brother; but I ſhould be glad to change
" the fubjeſt; what I have faid has been
" urged from me."—

" You

"You have been very hard upon the pro-
"feffion of a foldier," faid Sir Roger; "I
"hope my fweet Mabel has not imbibed
"your way of thinking."—"No, indeed,"
replied Mabel, "I am quite of a different
"opinion: I think a foldier the moft ho-
"nourable of all profeffions, and that all
"the great men, whofe names I always took
"pleafure to hear, were of it. I enjoyed
"my father's glory, and I hope to partake
"that of my hufband, though I expect to
"meet with pain and trouble in my way to
"it; but I hope to bear it with patience and
"fortitude. It is noble to devote one's felf
"to the fervice of one's country, to fuffer
"for it, and to die in the defence of it."—
"There I agree with you," replied Edith:
"to die in defence of one's country is a
"duty; but there is a great difference be-
"tween a war of offence and defence. To
"attack the dominions of other people, to
"wifh to conquer what is not our own, to
"take away what is the natural right of
"others, this appears to me cruel and un-
"juft: but to defend our own country when
"invaded by its enemies, this is juft and

"ne-

" neceſſary, and they do not deſerve its
" protection, that would not arm in defence
" of it."—

" There is much to be ſaid on both ſides
" of this argument," ſaid Lady Calverly;
" permit me to moderate between my daugh-
" ters, they are both right in ſome reſpects.
" A ſoldier cannot be allowed to reaſon
" upon the original cauſe of the war he is
" engaged in; he muſt fight for his king
" and country, and pray that their cauſe
" may be always united; but at the ſame
" time I agree with my Edith, that a ſol-
" dier's wife has much to ſuffer; I ſpeak
" from experience. When Sir Hugh Cal-
" verly was Governor of Calais, I was with
" him at the time it was attacked by the
" French. My huſband defended it gal-
" lantly, he forced his enemies to quit the
" ſiege of it. He acquired honour and
" glory, but what did his wife and children
" ſuffer during the time of the ſiege? I was
" not ſo great a heroine as willingly to ſa-
" crifice my huſband to his glory, nor ſo un-
" worthy an Engliſhwoman, as to wiſh him
" to ſave his life at the expence of his ho-
" nour

"nour and character. It is this ftruggle
"that makes the fituation fo truly painful;
"it is our duty to fubmit to it, and we can
"only wifh and pray for a happy event. I
"do not blame my Edith's refolution, ex-
"cept in what concerns myfelf; far be it
"from me to wifh her to live fingle upon
"my account, yet I am truly fenfible of
"the facrifice fhe offers me; fhe is the beft
"and deareft of children, my friend, my
"comforter, my counfellor; but I will part
"with her at any time to promote her inte-
"reft and happinefs."—

"My happinefs," faith Edith, "is beft
"promoted by that of my mother; I will
"never leave her while I live. I wifh my
"brother and friends to know it, that I may
"never more be afked to do it; for the reft,
"it is better that people fhould differ in
"opinion upon every fubje? ; there will
"always be found men enough to purfue
"what is called glory, ambition, prefer-
"ment; the few who do not choofe thefe
"paths, may fit down contented in obfcu-
"rity without being miffed or wanted. I
"am one of thefe, and I may enjoy my own

K 3   "wifhes,

" wifhes, without interfering with thofe of
" others."—

Lady Calverly made a motion to retire,
her daughters followed her, they purfued
the fubjeƈt in their own apartment. Mabel's fentiments were heroic and great;
Edith's were humble and rural, fhe preferred
content in a cottage. My Lady was of opinion that both were right in their refpeƈtive
fituations. In her youth fhe had talked
much of honour and glory, but in after life
fhe preferred eafe and content.

The gentlemen rode out and did not return till the hour of fupper.

Mr. Ralph Baffet rode next Sir John Calverly, and in the courfe of their converfation he fpoke of his intended fuit to Edith.
" Your fifter, Sir John, is a charming lady;
" but fhe difcourages every man who pretends
" to her, and tells them beforehand that
" their fuit will be unfuccefsful."—

. " That is true, Sir; my mother and fhe
" have the moft entire friendfhip for each
" other; they choofe to live together, and I
" cannot prevail upon myfelf to endeavour
" to feparate them. I am fenfible of the ho-

" nour

" nour you do our family, and fhould be
" happy to call you brother; but I can only
" propofe it, I cannot encourage you farther.
" I pleafed myfelf in my own marriage, I
" cannot urge my fifter to accept any man;
" yet I wifh her happily married: but after
" what you have heard, you cannot hope to
" fucceed with her; if you ftill wifh me to
" propofe it, I will do it."—" I beg you will,
" Sir; I will make one attempt, and if I
" find fhe cannot love me, I will defift, for
" her fake, and for my own."—

The conference ended here; the gentlemen took their circuit, and returned in health
and fpirits to meet the ladies at fupper.

Sir Roger de Clarendon revived the fubject begun after dinner.

He fpoke in praife of a military life; he
drew the character of a perfect hero, and
then inftanced the characters of the great
King Edward the Third and of his fon Edward Prince of Wales; he expatiated upon
their merits in every point of view, as men,
as princes, as warriors, as ftatefmen, as hufbands and fathers, and concluded by remark-
ing, that no man in a ftate of contented ob-

fcurity

fcurity could have opportunity to fhow forth' thofe virtues, which an active life brought forward to view, and put into employment. Sir John faid, that the late reign was an æra of heroes; the example of the King and Prince raifed an army of fuch men, and they might enumerate them till they grew tired of fpeaking; that many were ftill living who were worthy of a place in the lift of famous men of our times.

Mr. Clement Woodville drew a paper out of his pocket, faying, " I have here a lift " of famous men living in the reign of Ed- " ward the Third; but before I read it, per- " mit me to obferve, that heroes muft eat as " well as other men, and therefore they " ought not to defpife or opprefs thofe who " by their labours fupply all their wants, " and befide by the comparifon give them " moft of their advantages, and alfo fupport " their glory. Such are the farmers, gra- " ziers, hufbandmen, mechanics, artificers, " &c. Without thefe, heroes would be " like princes without fubjects to rule over; " thefe are the bulk of the people, for thefe " laws are made and properly fecured.
" When

"When heroes defend and protect them,
"they are truly glorious, but when they
"oppreſs and inſult them, they become the
"ſcourges of mankind, and a burthen to
"the world."—

"You ſpeak the truth," ſaid Mr. Thomas
Baſſet, "and I beg leave to mention an or-
"der of men which you have omitted, men
"of letters, without whom heroes and their
"actions would ſoon be forgotten : they are
"alſo mediators and miniſters of peace, as
"by their religion they ought always to be,
"though they ſometimes diſobey its com-
"mands. When the great King Edward
"lay with his army before Chartres, reſol-
"ving to be acknowledged King of France
"or to die in the field, the ambaſſadors of
"the Pope and the regent of France follow-
"ed him with offers of peace upon ſafe and
"honourable terms. Thomas the great and
"good Duke of Lancaſter remonſtrated
"earneſtly on the viciſſitudes of war, and
"the bleſſings of peace ; but ſtill the King
"was inflexible. There happened at that
"time an event the moſt remarkable, and,
"perhaps, miraculous ; for while the King

K 5   "ap-

" appeared inexorable, and refufed to hear the
" commiffioners of peace, there fell a moft
" terrible ftorm of thunder and lightning,
" rain and hail, upon the Englifh army,
" that feemed as if all nature was near its
" diffolution. Horfes and men were killed
" in their ranks to the number of above a
" thoufand of each, among whom where the
" noble Lord Guy Beauchamp, eldeft fon to
" the Earl of Warwick, and Robert Lord
" Morley. The boldeft hearts among thofe
" heroes trembled, and looked upon this
" tempeft as a mark of the divine difpleafure.
" The King was ftruck with awe and reve-
" rence, he kneeled upon the earth unco-
" vered, and made a folemn vow to God
" that he would now liften to terms of
" peace, and accept them upon good condi-
" tions. By this conduct he obtained more
" true glory, than he could have done by an
" obftinate perfeverance in his firft refolu-
" tion, even if it had been crowned with
" fuccefs; and by his conduct fhewed, that
" peace is more defirable than war.

" Thofe who record the actions of princes,
" and of great men, fhould think it their
" ho-

" honour and their duty to point out the
" true motives of noble actions, to be such
" as proceed from piety and virtue, and not
" from base and venal confiderations, lead
" them to prefer the falfe glory to the true;
" therefore I fay, that men of letters, and of
" virtuous principles, are to be highly re-
" fpected by thofe of all other callings and
" profeffions.."—

Sir John Calverly next fpoke: " Gen-
" tlemen, you have all fpoken well in be-
" half of your refpective profeffions. Per-
" mit me to be the moderator between you.
" My brother Sir Roger has fupported the
" honour and glory of a military ftation;
" my friend Clement has been the advocate
" of peace and all its occupations; Mr.
" Thomas Baffet has well difplayed the ho-
" nour and utility of that profeffion to
" which he will prove an ornament: all
" thefe are neceffary, and are ufeful in a
" ftate, and neither of them fhould be too
" highly exalted at the expence of the others.
" I honour them all, and allow that the arts
" and employments of peace are the moft
" neceffary to the health and welfare of a

" ftate;

" ftate; but ftill I do not mean to underva-
" lue the profeffion of arms, its labours, or
" its glories. The wifeft and beft of princes
" have thought it neceffary to employ high
" and turbulent fpirits in this way, for their
" own benefit, and that of their country.
" They have remarked, that in time of peace
" fuch fpirits as I have mentioned, will be
" bufy and factious at home, wherefore it is
" beft to keep their minds and bodies exer-
" cifed, and in conftant readinefs whenever
" their country fhall ftand in need of their
" fervices. Moreover, foreign princes and
" potentates will be more likely to preferve
" peace, when they fee us ready prepared for
" war.

" I could mention many other circum-
" ftances in behalf of the military profef-
" fion, that men of the greateft valour have
" alfo fhewn the greateft humanity, and the
" moft polifhed manners; that many of
" them have been well fkilled in the arts of
" peace; that fome have been the recorders
" of their own actions, and thofe of others.
" We know that the great Cæfar wrote his
" own commentaries; and finally, that fol-
" diers

" diers may excel in many other kinds of
" knowledge, befide that of the duties of
" their profeffion."—

" Far be it from me," faid Clement Woodville, " to depreciate the profeffion of a fol-
" dier ; I only meant to affert, that it is not
" the only one that is refpectable. If I have
" feemed to undervalue it, I hope my lift of
" great men will make atonement, for mili-
" tary men ftand foremoft in it, as needs
" muft be when the King was fo great a
" warrior."—

The gentlemen called for it without farther delay. Clement began—" I fhall beg
" your permiffion, gentlemen, as I read the
" names, to make fome brief remarks upon
" the moft eminent characters. At the head
" of my catalogue I have placed our late
" moft famous King Edward the Third; Sir
" Roger has expatiated upon his merits as a
" warrior, he was the firft hero of his age ;
" but I fhall add, that his character in all
" other refpects is no way inferior. That he
" underftood all the arts of peace, that he
" was an encourager of the arts and fciences,
" of trade and commerce. A retrofpect of
" all

" all the acts of Parliament paffed in his
" reign, will afford fufficient teftimony of
" his juftice and prudence, fuch as will make
" his encomium defcend to late pofterity.

" I fhall conclude with the remark that he
" was the fooneft a man, and remained fo the
" longeft, of any prince in the annals of our
" country. He came to the throne in his fif-
" teenth year, he was an hufband and a fa-
" ther at eighteen, he reigned fifty-one years,
" and lived fixty-five.

" Next to him I have placed his eldeft
" fon, Edward Prince of Wales, whofe cha-
" racter and glorious actions ftill live in the
" memory of all men.

" He was taken from us too foon; the na-
" tion ftill feels his lofs, and fo does his fon
" alfo; if he had lived, he would have train-
" ed him up to all the duties and qualities of
" a king, but he was too foon his own maf-
" ter and our's. God fend that the fucceed-
" ing part of his reign may be more fortu-
" nate and happy than the paft!

" Lionel Duke of Clarence was the third
" fon in order of birth. He was a moft
" beautiful and accomplifhed prince, and
" had

" had given many proofs of his abilities both
" as a warrior and a ſtateſman. He died of
" a fever very ſoon after his ſecond marriage
" at Milan.

" John of Ghent, Duke of Lancaſter,
" fourth ſon, a Prince of the greateſt cou-
" rage and abilities, and of an high and am-
" bitious ſpirit, capable of the greateſt at-
" chievements, as all the world knows and
" teſtifies.

" He married to his firſt wife, the Lady
" Blanch, heireſs of the illuſtrious houſe of
" Lancaſter, deſcended from King Henry
" III. In right of her he became Duke of
" Lancaſter, Earl of Derby, Lincoln, and
" Leiceſter, Lord Bergerac, Beaufort, and
" Nogent in France, all which titles the
" King his father confirmed to him by pa-
" tent. His ſecond wife was the Princeſs
" Conſtance, eldeſt daughter of Don Pedro
" King of Spain, in whoſe right he claims
" the crowns of Caſtile and Leon, which are
" now enjoyed by Don Henry, baſtard bro-
" ther of her father, and choſen by the no-
" bility of that country. This conteſt hath
" coſt England dear, and though ceaſed for
" a time,

" a time, is not even yet given up. The Duke
" of Lancaſter was ſuſpected of aiming at
" the crown in the early part of the King's
" minority, but his conduct has cleared him
" of that charge. This Prince hath many
" enemies, I leave it to them to ſpeak of his
" faults.

" Edmund of Langley, Duke of York,
" fifth ſon; the character of this Prince is
" truly reſpectable, though he wants nei-
" ther courage nor abilities, they are em-
" ployed in mediating between contending
" princes and parties. The Duke of York
" is beloved and reſpected by all men, and
" even the King will liſten to him, when he
" refuſes to hear all others.

" Thomas of Woodſtock, Duke of Glo-
" ceſter, the ſixth ſon now living. A
" Prince of great virtue and abilities, and
" only one fault, that of too warm and open
" a temper, and ſometimes too free in re-
" proving the folly and miſconduct of un-
" worthy men, when in power and place.
" This renders him liable to the attacks of
" his enemies, who whiſper calumnies in the
" ears of the King, who liſtens to them too
" rea-

" readily. No man living is more refpected
" by all true lovers of their country, than
" is the Duke of Gloucefter. He married
" the Lady Catherine, daughter of Hum-
" phry Bohun, Earl of Northampton.
" Mary, the other daughter and co-heirefs,
" was married to Henry Plantagenet, eldeft
" fon of John Duke of Lancafter, and in
" his wife's right Earl of Hereford, and from
" his father's gift Earl of Derby.——

" The daughters of King Edward the
" Third were married to men worthy of
" fuch alliance. Ifabel the eldeft, to Ingel-
" ram, Lord Coucy, a man of high fame
" and renown; the Princefs and he loved
" each other many years before they were
" permitted to marry, but foon after he was
" created Earl of Bedford, and Lord of
" ————, in Ireland.

" Joanna, the fecond daughter, was con-
" tracted to the Prince of Spain; going over
" to confummate her marriage, fhe died on
" her journey.

" Blanche, the third daughter, died in her
" infancy. Mary, fourth daughter, mar-
" ried to John, the valiant Duke of Bre-
" tagne.

" tagne. Mary, fifth daughter, married
" John Haſtings, Earl of Pembroke.

" Seldom ſhall we hear of a royal family
" ſo numerous and flouriſhing, nor ſo de-
" ſerving of honour, as the offspring of our
" King Edward the Third.

" The princes of the blood royal are
" likewiſe worthy to be mentioned in our
" liſt of great men, all of them worthy of
" the name of Plantagenet.

" And firſt, John of Eltham, the King's
" only brother, created by him Duke of,
" Cornwall. He diſtinguiſhed himſelf in an
" expedition to Scotland, and died there in
" the flower of his youth, truly beloved and
" lamented by his brother and all his rela-
" tions.

" Thomas of Brotherton, Earl of Nor-
" folk, and Edmund of Wodeſtoke, Earl of
" Kent, ſons of Edward the Firſt, by his
" ſecond wife Margaret of France, and bro-
" thers of Edward the Second.

" The firſt of theſe Princes left only one
" daughter, married to John Lord Seagrave;
" ſhe left a daughter likewiſe called Anne,
" married to John Lord Mowbray, who in
" her

" her right is Earl of Norfolk, and Earl
" Marſhal of England. The ſecond bro-
" ther, Earl of Kent, was treacherouſly be-
" trayed and brought to the ſcaffold, by the
" arts of Mortimer Earl of March, during
" the late King's minority. After the King
" took the reins of government into his own
" hands, Mortimer received his deſerts.
" The ſons of the Earl of Kent were re-
" ſtored to their rights, and were ſucceſ-
" ſively Earls of Kent : they dying without
" heirs, their titles and their fortunes de-
" ſcended to their only ſiſter Joanna, firſt
" married to Thomas Lord Holland, and
" ſecondly, to the noble Prince of Wales,
" and ſhe became the mother of our preſent
" King.

" The illuſtrious houſe of Plantagenet
" may challenge all the world to ſhow more
" great men, or more worthy to ſtand
" foremoſt in the liſts of fame.

" I ſhall next mention the names of ſuch
" eminent men as lived in the reign of our
" King Edward, eſpecially thoſe who ſhared
" his labours and his glory."—

" Stop

"Stop awhile and take breath," faid Sir John Calverly; "I am inclined to remark "upon fome of thofe you have already "named. I agree with you in regard to "moft of them; but if we fpeak of the cha-"racters of men, we fhould not magnify "their virtues, and conceal their faults; "we owe this juftice to ourfelves and to "pofterity."—

"Have I done fo in any inftance, Sir "John? If I have, I beg you to correct "me."—

"I think you have in your account of the "Duke of Lancafter; after fetting forth his "virtues, you leave it to his enemies to fhew "his faults. I am not one of thefe, yet I "think them abatements of his character, "and I will venture in this company to "mention fome of the moft confiderable. "In the firft place, his ambition is unbound-"ed, aiming at fovereign power, and ftri-"ving to involve this country in war and "troubles, in order to fet the crown of Spain "upon his head. Secondly, his pride is fo "great, that he thinks himfelf fuperior to "all men, and entitled to all the homage due

"to

" to fovereign princes. Thirdly, he has de-
" graded himfelf and the royal family. Af-
" ter being married to two princeffes of the
" firft rank and dignity, he took to wife an
" obfcure woman, whom he had publicly
" kept as his concubine during the life of
" his fecond lady, and by whom he had three
" fons and a daughter then living. He pre-
" vailed on the Pope to legitimate thefe chil-
" dren, and gave them the rank of princes
" of the blood. The real princes of the
" family would not fuffer them to affume
" the name of Plantagenet, fo they took
" that of Beaufort from the caftle where
" they were born. The ladies of the blood
" royal refufed to appear in public with their
" mother, and the nobility thought them-
" felves affronted by her taking place of their
" families, many of which are allied to the
" throne. Thefe things have juftly leffen-
" ed the Duke in the eyes of all men."—

" Permit me to fay a few words on the
" other fide," faid Sir Roger de Clarendon.
" All great characters have their allay, and
" much allowance is due to fo great a man ;
" all Europe celebrates his name as one of
" the

" the firſt warriors and ſtateſmen, and all the
" courts in it have always treated him with
" the higheſt reſpect, not excepting that of
" France."——

Mr. T. Baſſet next ſpoke upon this ſubject.——" Certainly the Duke is a man of
" many noble and princely virtues : he is
" noble, generous, and wiſe : a great war-
" rior and politician. He is alſo the patron
" of learned and ingenious men, and a liberal
" rewarder of all kinds of merit."——

" All that has been ſaid is true," ſaid Mr.
Ralph Baſſet, " and our friend Sir John has
" ſaid nothing that is not equally ſo. But
" when we give or receive the characters of
" great men, we ſhould weigh their virtues
" and their defects likewiſe, to form a true
" eſtimate of them.

" If men were ſecure that their virtues
" would be celebrated, and their faults con-
" cealed or ſlightly paſſed over, they would
" think they might be excuſed for whatever
" bad actions they could commit. Princes
" ought to lie under this check as well as
" other men, leſt their pride ſhould run to
" too high a pitch ; they ought to be told,
" that

" that however the voice of praife or flattery
" may fpeak of them while living, their true
" characters will certainly be known after
" their death, and the higher their fituation,
" the more their qualities will be invefti-
" gated.

" This truth being rightly underftood,
" would make them careful of their every
" action, and confider themfelves as account-
" able to pofterity."—

" You have well fpoken," faid Sir John
Calverly, " and I am pleafed to have led
" the way to fuch pertinent and ufeful ob-
" fervations."—

Mr. Woodville apologized for his omif-
fion, faying, it was owing to a defire of bre-
vity, that he had omitted many obvious remarks; but he agreed with the gentlemen
who had fpoken after him, and that he
fhould defer the remainder of his lift to fome
other time.

Lady Calverly made a motion to retire,
but begged Clement to referve the remainder of his lift till fhe and her daughters
fhould be prefent.

I

Sir

Sir John Calverly ·fixed the next evening to purfue the fubject; and the company feparated at a later hour than ufual.

The next day Mr. Ralph Baffet made propofals to Lady Calverly for her daughter Edith: he confeffed that her declaration had made him doubtful whether to offer himfelf or not, but his refpect for the family and the pleafure he had enjoyed in their company, had counteracted the blow that her coldnefs had ftruck him, 'and he ardently wifhed to be her fon, and the brother of Sir John Calverly. My Lady faid, fhe muft refer him entirely to her daughter. " You " have heard, I prefume, that my daughter " Mabel chofe a hufband for herfelf without " my knowledge : it is true, it was a man " whom I could not but approve; but after " allowing of her choice, I could not refufe " the fame privilege to Edith, who is my " beft child, my friend, and my counfellor; " fhe deferves to be the miftrefs of her own " deftiny, and fhe fhall be fo. If fhe ac- " cepts your propofal, I fhall give my warm " confent; but if fhe declines it, I fhall not " urge her in your behalf. I deal plainly " with

" with you, Sir, and I hope you will take it
" as a proof of my fincerity and refpect for
" you."—

Mr. Baffet afked an interview with Edith;
fhe did not decline it.

He offered himfelf to her difpofal; fhe
gave a decided negative, but faid, " Though
" I do not accept you for my hufband, I
" wifh to retain you as my friend; I refpect
" your family, I like your company, and
" your brother's alfo. You are Sir Roger's
" friend, fuffer me to call you mine. I
" had hoped that my whimfical declaration
" would have fpared me the pain of giving
" you a refufal; but now that is over, and I
" hope you will never more urge the repeti-
" tion."—He wifhed her to receive his vifits, and to be a candidate for her favour;
fhe pofitively forbad it.

He told her he muft then leave the houfe
directly. She told him, " No, you muft
" not. I invite you to ftay and purfue the
" fubject to which you did honour laft
" night; you muft ftay till it is concluded."—

She looked with fo much fweetnefs and
complacency, that Mr. Baffet could not de-

cline her invitation, though mortified by
her refusal.

He sought his friend Sir Roger de Clarendon, and told him of the repulse he had
met with, and the invitation that had followed it. He advised him to accept the invitation, and to put aside the repulse. " I
" will found the depth for you, and then'
" tell you whether to persevere or to re-
" treat."—

Sir Roger invited Edith to walk with him
in the garden; he led her to the alcove
where he had first opened his heart to Mabel: he expatiated upon the beauties of it,
and wished it might ever be propitious to
lovers. He then spoke in behalf of his
friend, he enlarged upon his merits, and be-
sought her to consider and to know him better, before she condemned him to despair.—
Edith was cool and resolute; she said little,
and that only to confirm the negative she
had given. Sir Roger looked earnestly at
her, he said, " My sweet sister, be sincere
" with me; have you not made a choice in
" your heart that renders all the rest of man-
" kind indifferent to you?"—Edith blushed,

but

but tried to parry the ftroke; fhe told him
he was not her confeffor, and fhe would not
tell him. He faid, " Do not I know a man in
" whom meet all the requifites you expect in
" a hufband? A man of peace, amiable, gen-
" tle, virtuous, and engaging?"—She blufhed and looked down: he proceeded; " A
" man beloved by all that know him; one
" whom I have chofen for my friend, one
" whom Lady Calverly efteems, and whom
" fhe trufts, and Sir John already loves him
" as a brother."—Edith turned afide; fhe
was confufed, fhe ftrove to recover her
ufual prefence of mind, but found fhe could
not: fhe was filent fome moments.--"Enough,
" my deareft lady; forgive my impertinent
" curiofity. I wifh to ferve you, and to
" ferve him; only tell me how I can do it,
" and defpife me if I do not undertake it."—
    Edith then fpoke—" The only favour I
" afk of you, Sir Roger, is to keep your
" fufpicions to yourfelf, and above all things
" not to utter them before my mother or
" my brother."—" It furprifes me that they
" do not fufpect it; you drew your lover's
" picture well, there was no occafion to put

" his

" his name to it ; but I knew it before.
" Lovers the foonest find out lovers, and I
" had found out Clement. I will, how-
" ever, obey your commands ; but why is
" this the only favour you will accept of
" me ? I have fome interest at court, I
" would ufe it to ferve our dear friend : I
" had intended to invite him to go with us
" to Ireland, but you do not love a foldier,
" you will have only a man of peace."—

Edith coloured—" I do not wifh my
" friend to decline the fervice ; if the King
" calls him to this or any other employment,
" he has too much honour and fpirit to re-
" fufe to attend on his commands. I fhould
" be grieved and afhamed to have it thought
" that I would hinder him."—" There fpoke
" the daughter of Sir Hugh Calverly ; would
" you, then, wifh me to invite him ?"—

" Certainly, Sir ; I fhall never oppofe
" any thing that is for Mr. Woodville's
" honour and advantage."—

" Will you honour me with any other
" commands ?"—

" Yes, one more ; do not fuffer Mr. Baf-
" fet to fufpect."—" I will not ; but I will
" ad-

" advife him to give up all his hopes."——
" I thank you; that will, indeed, oblige
" me highly."——

Sir John and Mr. Baffet entered the garden; they met them, and the converfation
became general.——

LITERARY ASSEMBLY,
OLD BOND-STREET.

Under the Patronage of their Royal Highnesses
THE PRINCE OF WALES,
DUKE OF YORK,
DUKE OF CLARENCE,
DUKE OF GLOUCESTER,
HIS HIGHNESS PRINCE-WILLIAM FREDERIC,
AND MANY OF THE PRINCIPAL NOBILITY AND
GENTRY.

HOOKHAM,

Whose most strenuous exertions have been uniformly and unremittedly directed to promote the interest of society, and the encouragement and dissemination of Literature, has, at a very great expence, fitted up an elegant suit of apartments for the establishment of a

LITERARY ASSEMBLY,

Which he daily furnishes with the various Publications of this and every foreign country, on all subjects; and including all the Periodical and Diurnal Productions of repute to be met with on the Continent, in GREAT

BRI-

Britain and Ireland, the East and West Indies, as well as the Foreign Gazettes.

His plan having received, independent of particular patronage, the fanction of the public approbation, and his very refpectable Lift of Subfcribers already convincing him that he was not too fanguine when he projected it, he now intends to folicit the more immediate attention of Men of Letters and Travellers. It is to fuch he looks for its fupport, and from fuch he hopes for that information which will tend to its perfection. Whatever improvement they may pleafe to fuggeft fhall be thankfully adopted.

It is his higheft ambition to render his Literary Assembly a centre of general communication, where perfons of curiofity may find the beft company, the beft books, the beft intelligence, with the beft accommodations. He is confident, that when the fcale and aim of his Plan are fully known, it will be found beneficial to the community at large, and extremely convenient to all who have occafion to confult a library, or who wifh to have the occurrences of the day, as it is the moft extenfive inftitution of the kind ever attempted, and as he, though at an age when men moft claim the privilege of retreating from bufinefs, will not confider it

as

as complete till it furnishes every possible aid to Literature, and is deemed as much an honour to his Country, as his

CIRCULATING LIBRARY,

Now for thirty years established, has been a benefit to it.——The Subscription to the LITERARY ASSEMBLY will be TWO GUINEAS per ann. which, he is convinced, will not be thought extravagant, considering the immense number of publications daily issuing from the press.

As it is his wish to have the Company as select as possible, none but Subscribers can be admitted, nor any person as a Subscriber, unless introduced by a Member, or known to HOOKHAM; but as many respectable FOREIGNERS whose residence may not exceed three months, may wish, during that time, to see the GAZETTES of their respective countries, they also will be admitted, for that period, by the introduction of a Member, on paying One Guinea.

The Rooms are opened at TEN in the Morning, every Day, Sunday excepted, and shut at the same hour in the evening.

*** No Book, Pamphlet, or Newspaper, can be allowed to be taken out of the room.

www.ingramcontent.com/pod-product-compliance
Lightning Source LLC
Chambersburg PA
CBHW030814020726
47499CB00006B/1907